First Dibs

Mom said she couldn't wait to see the puppies.
Dad said not to choose one because it wasn't settled yet. Then Chad remembered he had forgotten to claim first dibs. He grabbed his toast and
hurried back to the Garcias'. But it was too late.
Leslie was standing on the Garcias' front walk,
grinning. "I got first dibs, Chad Abernathy! I get
to choose first!"

FUDGE

Charlotte Towner
Graeber

illustrated by Cheryl Harness

A MINSTREL® BOOK

PUBLISHED BY POCKET BOOKS

New York   London   Toronto   Sydney   Tokyo

*For my son, Scot,
and in memory of my dogs
Casey, Klinker, and Heidie*

A Minstrel Book published by
POCKET BOOKS, a division of Simon & Schuster Inc.,
1230 Avenue of the Americas, New York, NY 10020

Published by arrangement with Lothrop, Lee & Shepard Books,
a division of William Morrow & Company, Inc.
Library of Congress Catalog Card Number: 86-7353

ISBN: 0-671-67384-X

First Minstrel Books Printing June, 1988

10 9 8 7 6 5 4 3 2

A MINSTREL BOOK and colophon are registered trademarks of Simon & Schuster Inc.

Printed in the U.S.A.

1

"**C**had, don't gulp your cereal. School doesn't start until eight-thirty," Mom said.

Chad looked at the kitchen clock and ate faster. Biggie, the Garcias' brown Labrador retriever, was ready to have her puppies, and Chad wanted to check on her before school.

"What's the rush?" Dad asked. "It's only five after."

"It's Biggie," Mom said. "Chad doesn't want to miss the big event."

"I just want to see if Biggie's had her puppies yet," Chad explained. "Mrs. Garcia said they might be born during the night."

Mom patted her stomach. "I wish Baby Abernathy were due now instead of the end of October. Then I wouldn't be rushing off to work, and Chad could stay home this summer instead of going to the Garcias' every day." She arched her back. "Baby Abernathy must be a giant—I look like a barn already."

Chad thought Mom looked okay—her stomach stuck out like a soccer ball, but not like a barn. And he didn't mind going over to the Garcias' while Mom worked at the bank. The Garcias lived right across the street, and Tomas Garcia was his best friend. Best of all, the Garcias owned Biggie—Chad's favorite dog in the whole world.

"Baby Abernathy will be here before we know it," Dad said, laughing. "Then we'll be rushing around both day and night. Right now I've got to rush off to my switch plates and fuses." He rinsed his dishes at the sink and gave Mom a hug. Chad did the same, grabbed his lunch box, and hurried across Franklin Street.

In the Garcias' kitchen Tomas, his sister Anna, and Little Joe were still eating breakfast. Mrs. Garcia was combing Carmella's long hair in the living room.

"No puppies yet," Mrs. Garcia said when

Chad asked about Biggie. "But you can go out to see her if you're quiet."

Chad headed for the porch at the rear of the house. Last Saturday Mrs. Garcia had placed a rug and old blankets on the porch floor. Mr. Garcia had fixed the porch door so Biggie could go in and out whenever she needed to. And yesterday Chad and Tomas had made a sign for Biggie's porch corner. "Quiet—Puppies' Room," it said. The sign had been Chad's idea. At home Mom and Dad were already calling the spare room "the baby's room."

Now Biggie lay on the blankets with her eyes closed. For a moment Chad stood in the doorway, watching. Then he crossed the porch and sat down beside her. Gently he pushed his fingers through Biggie's thick hair. "How are you doing, Biggie?" Chad asked.

The big Lab opened her eyes, groaned with pleasure, and put one paw on Chad's knee. Just then Chad felt a familiar *thump a bump a bump* against his arm, and he knew that inside Biggie's body the puppies were moving around, stretching, and growing.

The first time Chad had felt the move-

ments, a month ago, it had been scary. He and Tomas had been reading comic books in the Garcias' backyard. Biggie had been on the ground beside them, with Chad leaning against her. When Chad had felt the strange quivers against his knee, he had jumped away.

"Tomas," he had said, "Biggie's stomach is moving!"

Tomas had nodded. "The puppies are kicking. If you put your hand on her stomach, you can feel."

After that Chad had often felt the puppies move. When they were still, Tomas said they were sleeping. When they kicked hard, he said they were exercising.

At home Baby Abernathy was moving around too. Chad put his hand on Mom's shirt front one evening and felt little *thump a bump*s against his palm. Mom said the movements meant that the baby was exercising like Biggie's puppies.

This morning the puppies' *thump a bump*s felt stronger than ever. Chad smoothed Biggie's soft ears. "Good girl, pretty girl," he said.

Then it was time to leave for school. Tomas, Carmella, and Anna scrambled out with lunch boxes and books. Chad closed the porch door and joined them.

"Tie your shoes, Anna!" Mrs. Garcia called from the doorway. She grabbed Little Joe as he tried to duck outside.

They were halfway to school when Leslie Patterson hollered, "Wait up!" and everyone turned. Leslie was lugging an old briefcase under one arm as she ran toward them. It was covered with stickers of cats and unicorns.

Chad and Tomas walked ahead of the girls. But Chad heard what they were saying. Leslie was asking about the puppies. "Are they born yet?" she squealed. Then she said, "First dibs! I get first dibs on Biggie's puppies!"

Chad spun around. He had thought about owning one of Biggie's puppies, but he hadn't asked Mom and Dad about it yet. The puppies weren't even born.

"First dibs aren't fair until the puppies are born!" he shouted. "Besides, I'll bet you can't even have one!" Chad remembered Leslie's mother giving away Leslie's kitten, Sneeze, last winter. Mrs. Patterson didn't like pets much, Chad thought.

Leslie flipped her bangs. "My father likes dogs. And he wants a big one, too."

Chad hurried to catch up with Tomas. Mom and Dad *both* liked dogs, especially Biggie. Mom saved bones for her, and Dad played catch with her in the alley. Mom and Dad had talked about getting a dog like Biggie someday, and Chad thought one of Biggie's puppies would be perfect.

Biggie did not have her puppies that day. But at supper Chad asked about getting one. Mom was scooping salad into wooden bowls. Dad was shaking the bottle of French dressing.

"Mom . . . Dad," Chad began, "can we buy one of Biggie's puppies?"

Mom's look was steady. "I *knew* this was coming, Chad, but the puppies aren't born yet."

"Why the rush?" Dad asked, drizzling dressing on his salad.

"I want first dibs," he said. "Before Leslie."

"I see," Mom said.

"Leslie—I might have guessed," Dad said.

"Well, can we have one?" Chad asked.

Mom rested her elbows on the table, facing Dad. "I'll be quitting at the bank in August," she said. "Chad will be home from school. It might be a good time to train a puppy."

"Before Baby Abernathy is born?" Dad worried. "You've been tired lately, and puppies are a lot of work."

Chad didn't know about training a puppy —they had never had a dog. He had had a gerbil, once, that Mom had had to take care of when he forgot. Chad didn't remind Mom about Gerby.

"I remember Casey," Mom said dreamily. Then she started talking about the dog she and Uncle Stephen had had as children. "Every kid should have a dog like Casey."

Finally Dad said, "Wait until the puppies are born, Chad. Then we'll decide."

Chad settled to eating his salad. When Mom got dreamy about something, it was practically decided. He would claim first dibs the minute the puppies were born. Leslie would have to take second.

Biggie's puppies were born on the last day of school. Chad was getting dressed when Tomas banged at the front door. "Chad! Biggie is having her puppies!" he shouted. "Hurry!"

Chad ran across Franklin Street in his stocking feet. On the Garcias' porch Biggie lay on her blankets with four brown puppies squirming against the curve of her stomach.

"Aren't they cute, Chad?" Carmella whispered. She and Anna sat at the edge of the blankets with Little Joe in front of them.

"Don't crowd too close," Mrs. Garcia warned.

Mr. Garcia pulled Little Joe to the side. "Biggie needs room. There are more puppies coming."

"How many, Mama?" Anna asked.

Mrs. Garcia shrugged. "Three, maybe four."

Chad joined Tomas by the windows and watched the newborn puppies push and shove for their mother's milk. Their eyes were closed, and they made funny noises as they drank— like the squeaky toys that are sold at pet stores.

Chad was watching when the fifth puppy was born. Biggie groaned and began to pant, and suddenly the puppy popped out. The puppy was enclosed in a watery sac and attached to Biggie by a rubbery cord. Immediately Biggie bit through the sac and cord, cleaned the puppy with her rough tongue, and pushed it toward the others.

"Gee," Anna said, and Carmella sighed deeply. Little Joe touched the newest puppy on the head.

"Good girl, Biggie," Mrs. Garcia said, rubbing Biggie's ears. Biggie groaned and closed her eyes again.

Chad didn't say anything. He had never seen puppies—or any animals—born before. When Gerby had had her babies, she had hidden her nest inside an empty milk carton.

Mr. Garcia looked at his watch. "Time to get rolling," he said. "And kids, Biggie needs to rest." He lifted Little Joe from the floor and carried him into the house.

Mrs. Garcia scooted Anna and Carmella toward the kitchen. "You don't want to be late on the last day of school."

Chad hurried home to put on his shoes and to tell Mom and Dad about the puppies. "Five of them so far, and they're all like Biggie," he said.

Mom said she couldn't wait to see them. Dad said not to choose one because it wasn't settled yet. Then Chad remembered he had forgotten to claim first dibs. He grabbed his toast and hurried back to the Garcias'. But it was too late. Leslie was standing on the Garcias' front walk, grinning. "I got first dibs, Chad Abernathy! I get to choose first!"

2

No one expected it, but Biggie had eleven puppies in all. When Chad and Tomas came in from school, they were all sleeping in a heap. Carmella and Anna were already naming them.

"The big one should be named Biggie Two," Anna said. "She looks just like Biggie."

"They all look like Biggie," Carmella argued. "And what if she is a *he*?"

"Mama! Which puppies are girls?" Anna called.

Mrs. Garcia stepped onto the porch carrying a large pan of dog food. "Children, quiet!" she said. "Biggie's had a hard day." She placed the pan in front of Biggie and leaned down to rub Biggie's ears. "Good girl. Good mama dog."

Biggie looked worn out as she raised her head to eat. But she thumped her tail against the floor when her puppies squealed. And every few bites she stopped eating to nudge them close.

Chad hunkered down to get a closer look. Tomas had said there were eleven—six males and five females. At first, Chad counted only ten. Then he spotted a puppy hidden by Biggie's tail. It was smaller than the rest and darker brown in color. Chad didn't see how it could survive, being so small. He didn't see how Biggie could manage all eleven puppies at once. But Biggie nudged the smaller puppy toward the others, and it began to eat.

Like Anna, Chad wondered which puppies were male and which female. They were all chocolate brown, like Biggie. They all had pink noses and pink pads on their feet. The main difference was in their sizes. The big puppy was almost twice as big as the smallest one.

Chad was counting them again when Leslie sailed into the Garcias' backyard on her skate-

QUIET
PUPP/s
ROOM

board. She clattered onto the enclosed porch and parked her skateboard by the door.

"Oh, they're so cute," she cooed as she squeezed between Carmella and Anna. "They look like little brown bears."

"Teddy bears!" Anna said. "Let's name the big puppy Teddy Bear!"

Chad groaned, and Tomas snickered. Then Mr. Garcia came home from the lumberyard, and Little Joe woke up from his nap. It was time for Chad to go home. He and Leslie left the porch together.

"I think I like the big puppy best," Leslie said. "But I'm not sure. The smallest one is awfully cute."

Chad shrugged. With eleven puppies, it didn't matter that Leslie had first dibs. There were plenty to choose from. But Chad hoped Leslie wouldn't choose the smallest one. Leslie was rough, sometimes. She had hauled her kitten, Sneeze, around like a sack of beans. She had dressed it up in baby clothes and fed it from a bottle.

The next day Chad talked Mom and Dad into crossing the street to the Garcias'. "You've got to see the puppies," he urged. "They look just like Biggie."

Mr. Garcia met them at the porch door, and Mom oohed and aahed over each puppy. "So many, and they're all wonderful," she said.

"They're pedigreed," Mr. Garcia stated proudly. "The father is a show dog, Siegfried the Fourth. We have papers."

Dad explained that "papers" meant the puppies would be registered as purebred Labrador retrievers, like Biggie. The way Mr. Garcia spoke, Chad knew that was special.

"They're wonderful!" Mom said again as Mr. Garcia handed her one of the puppies. It was the smallest one. It was sleeping and lay contented in Mom's hands. Biggie raised her head to watch, but didn't protest. Mom closed her eyes as she nuzzled the puppy against her cheek.

When they were ready to leave, Dad winked at Mom. "Put our name on the list," he told Mr. Garcia. "When the puppies are old enough, we'll take one." Then he handed Mr. Garcia a twenty-dollar bill from his billfold as a deposit.

"Yay!" Chad yelled.

"Yay! Yay!" Tomas, Anna, and Carmella cheered.

At the door Chad looked back at Biggie and her puppies. It would be hard to choose one—they were all special. The big one was on top of the heap. All were squealing and grunting for Biggie's milk. The little puppy was squealing the loudest.

Although school was out for the summer, every weekday morning Chad got up early. He ate breakfast with Mom and Dad. Then he crossed the street to the Garcias', where he stayed while Mom was at work.

As soon as Chad got to the Garcias', he headed for the porch. First he greeted Biggie and made sure the little puppy was all right. Once he found it under Biggie's neck. He worried that it might get smothered, so he pulled it out. Sometimes the larger puppies pushed the little puppy away from Biggie's milk. Chad worried that it would not get enough to eat. So he pushed it close again.

"Don't worry, Chad," Mrs. Garcia said. "I'll keep a close watch on the little one."

The puppies were growing fast. In two weeks

their eyes were open—wonderful amber-brown eyes, like Biggie's. Chad knew now that the big puppy was a male. The small puppy was a female, and when Chad held her, she nuzzled against him.

Soon the puppies were moving around, squirming off the blankets. They tumbled and sprawled and toppled over one another. Sometimes they were almost too much for Biggie, and Chad tried to help. He unscrambled the puppies when they crowded in to eat. He rescued the small puppy when the others got too rough. Then he held her on his lap and let her bite his fingers with her tiny teeth.

By now most of the puppies had names. Leslie called the big puppy Bear. Tomas named one puppy Napper because she was always sleeping. Carmella and Anna named three puppies Ziggie, Piggie, and Figgie to rhyme with Biggie. Little Joe even called one puppy Joe, after himself.

Mr. Garcia was calling the smallest puppy Runty. "Every litter of pups seems to have one runt," he said. "She'll probably be the last to go."

"It's a crummy name," Chad said. "Besides, she's not a runt. She's just as good as the others."

Mr. Garcia laughed. "Think of a better name, then, Chad. Poco? That means 'little' in Spanish."

Chad shook his head. In the end he named the puppy Fudge. "Fudge because she is fudgy brown," he explained. "And because everyone likes fudge brownies."

After that they all called the puppy Fudge or Fudgie. Except when Little Joe said it, it came out Fushie.

And after that Chad *knew* he wanted Fudge for his own dog. He had worried about her and fed her and played with her every day. Now he had named her.

One morning Mom said, "I can't wait to stay home and get ready for the baby. I want to paint the baby's room and sew new curtains and—"

"Get ready for the puppy," Chad interrupted. "Mrs. Garcia said the puppies can be sold when they're eight weeks old."

"Which puppy are we getting?" Dad asked. "They all look the same to me."

Chad saw Dad wink at Mom as she turned

from the counter where she was buttering toast.

"Fudge," Chad announced.

Chad wasn't sure which puppy Leslie would choose—*if* her parents agreed about getting a dog. But he thought she liked Bear best. Every day Leslie showed up at the Garcias' to see the puppies. She played with Bear the most.

"My mother says dogs get fleas and ticks and have to be taken to the vet all the time," Leslie worried.

"Biggie doesn't have fleas or ticks!" Tomas said.

"She only goes to the vet once a year," Carmella said.

"Then the vet gives her a shot so she can get her tag," Anna explained.

Leslie shrugged. "I know. But my mother says dogs shed on the furniture and sleep on the beds."

"Biggie sleeps on my bed," Tomas said.

"My dog will sleep on *my* bed," Chad said firmly. He imagined Fudge curled up by his pillow at night.

Leslie shook her head and her bangs flew. "My mother would have a fit."

For once Chad felt sorry for Leslie. Maybe she wouldn't get to take one of Biggie's pups at all. "What does your father say?" he asked.

"My father is in Pennsylvania on business. He said we would talk about getting one of Biggie's puppies when he gets home." She lifted both Bear and Fudge onto her lap.

Chad knew he was lucky that both Mom and Dad wanted one of Biggie's puppies. He was glad Dad had given Mr. Garcia a deposit. He reached across Leslie's knee for Fudge, but Leslie pushed his hand away.

"I still have first dibs, Chad!" she yelled. "You can't choose first!"

"Dibs don't count!" Chad shouted back. "We have a deposit on a puppy—you don't!"

Mrs. Garcia came out to the porch. "Children! What's going on out here?"

"Leslie thinks she owns the place," Tomas said.

"I have first dibs," Leslie said, almost sobbing.

Chad tried to explain. "I only wanted to pet *my dog* and she started yelling."

"We'll have no more arguing about Biggie's puppies," Mrs. Garcia said. Then she shooed everyone into the backyard.

Carmella and Anna tried to comfort Leslie. "Your father will let you have a puppy," Anna said.

"You don't want runty Fudge anyway," Carmella said.

"She's not a runt!" Chad shouted at them.

"Come on, Chad," Tomas urged. "Let's get out of here."

Chad thumbed his nose at Leslie as he followed Tomas to the alley. He didn't feel sorry for her anymore. She had wrecked the whole morning with her tantrum. And no matter what—she couldn't have Fudge!

3

When the puppies were six weeks old, Chad started making plans to bring Fudge home. He counted the money in the dinosaur bank on his dresser. Tyrannosaurus rex held thirteen dollars and thirty-four cents—more than enough to buy a collar and leash for Fudge. Chad had checked on the prices at the mall. He wanted a brown collar and leash to match Fudge's coloring.

Chad wished he hadn't told Tomas and the others.

"A brown leash and collar?" Tomas said. "I'd choose red." Tomas liked red—his bike was red, his school lunch box was red, he even had a red collar for Biggie.

"My sister, Jennifer, likes brown," Leslie said. "But I think brown is boring. *My* dog will have a pink collar and a purple leash."

Chad didn't tell Leslie he thought pink and purple looked ugly together. She was wearing a pink T-shirt with a purple unicorn on the front. Besides, her father and mother had not agreed about one of Biggie's puppies yet.

"Lots of good things are brown," Chad insisted. "Nuts and chocolate and brownies are brown." Across the Garcias' backyard Biggie's puppies were playing with an old sock. "Biggie and her puppies are brown," he added.

On Saturday Chad asked Dad to take him and Tomas to the library. "I want to check out some books on dogs," he said.

Tomas wanted a mystery book and a book about baseball. So after lunch Dad drove them both to the St. Charles Public Library near the center of town.

In the junior department Chad found one whole shelf of dog books. He picked out *Dog Training for Kids* and *Dogs, All About Them.* Then he found two books about Labrador retrievers. He checked out all four books with his library card.

Reading about dogs, especially Labs, was

interesting. "Did you know that Labrador retrievers like water?" he asked Mom. "In the old days they used Labrador retrievers to rescue people lost at sea."

"We'll have to take Fudge swimming when she is old enough," Mom said.

Chad asked Dad, "Did you know that a Labrador retriever won a national Frisbee championship three years in a row? Labrador retrievers make the best hunting dogs, too."

"I'm impressed," Dad said.

Mostly Chad read about how to train a puppy. He knew without reading that puppies needed to eat four or five times a day. Biggie's puppies were eating solid food now, and Chad helped Tomas mix Puppy Bright, the special puppy meal. "One cup of water to three cups of meal," the package said. Tomas and Chad mixed four pans full every feeding. It was fun to watch the puppies eat. Noses, paws, even tails went into the feeding pans. Chad made sure Fudge got her share. Then he and Tomas washed Fudge and the others off with wet paper towels.

Chad knew that puppies had to be housebroken, too. Every day Mrs. Garcia spread clean newspapers on the porch floor and carried the dirty ones out to the trash. By the end of the day the newspapers were soiled and had to be replaced again. Chad would have to train Fudge to go outside. The puppy training book told how.

Chad made a list of everything Fudge would need. She would need a special place to sleep at night. She would need her own food and water dishes. She would have to go to the vet for puppy shots and an examination.

Mom went to the medical center once a month for an examination. It was important for both Mom and Baby Abernathy. Each month Dr. Thompson listened to Baby Abernathy's heartbeat and made sure Mom was healthy too. Now it was time for Mom's July appointment.

"I'm going right after work," she told Chad and Dad that morning. "No telling when I'll get home if the doctor is running late."

"Don't worry, we'll make supper," Dad offered.

"Don't cook for an army," Mom warned. "I'm gaining too much weight."

Chad liked it when he and Dad cooked together. Dad always tied a dish towel around Chad's waist like a chef's apron. And Dad didn't worry about fixing vegetables or how many vitamins everything had. They just cooked things they liked best. That night Dad brought home everything for homemade pizza.

"We'll get it all ready, and pop it in the oven when Mom pulls into the driveway," Dad said.

"I get to roll the dough," Chad said. "You get to chop the onions."

The pizza was ready to bake at six o'clock. It was almost seven when Mom got home. Chad heard her car on the gravel drive.

"She'll be tired and hungry," Dad said as he slid the pizza into the oven. "She probably had a long wait in the doctor's office."

Chad nodded. Mom hated waiting. She hated waiting in line at the grocery store. She hated waiting for stamps at the post office. Mom would be crabby from waiting.

But Mom looked happy when she came in. Her cheeks were flushed and her eyes sparkled. She set her purse on the counter, sat down at the table, and kicked off her shoes. "What a day. What a day," she sighed dreamily.

"Pizza will be ready in twenty minutes," Dad announced.

"We made it from scratch," Chad said.

Mom didn't seem to hear them. "I'm still in a daze," she said. "What a day."

"Kathleen? Is everything all right?" Dad asked. Dad often called·Mom Kathleen when he was worried. Chad was getting worried too.

Suddenly Mom stood up. She walked to the window and took a deep breath. "Well, here goes. Get ready. I've got some big news."

"Big news?" Dad said. His forehead crinkled into a frown. "What did the doctor say? Are you all right? What's wrong?"

"John, I'm all right," Mom said, laughing. "And nothing's wrong—exactly." All at once she climbed onto a kitchen chair, cupped her hands to her mouth like a megaphone, and announced, "Now hear this! Dr. Thompson says there are *two* Baby Abernathys. We are going to have *twins*!"

"Twins!" Dad gasped.

"Twins!" Chad gulped.

"There are *two* heartbeats," Mom said. "Dr. Thompson definitely heard *two* heartbeats."

The oven timer went off and Dad set the pizza on a cutting board to cool. Then he helped Mom down from the chair. "Kathleen? Are you sure? Do you feel all right?"

Mom sat down at the table and sighed. "Well, I have to quit working as soon as possible. Dr. Thompson says I have to stay off my feet until the babies are born. And I can't lift anything heavy or climb stairs," Mom said. "Otherwise I'm fine."

Dad asked a dozen questions more—why Mom had to take it easy, was there something wrong, should she see a specialist? Then he said, "It won't be so bad. We'll work it out."

"I'm carrying twins at thirty-five," Mom said. "I'm not a youngster anymore." She cut a piece of pizza but didn't eat it. Instead she blew her nose on a paper napkin.

Chad patted Mom's arm. "You're not old, Mom," he said. "Grandma Olsen is *old*, and even Mrs. Garcia is thirty-eight."

"Oh, Chad." Mom laughed and blew her nose again.

Then Chad told her his plan to buy Fudge a collar and leash. "I want everything brown like Fudge."

"The puppy!" Mom cried. "Oh, Chad, I forgot all about Fudge." She turned to Dad. "John, how can we manage the puppy *now*?"

Chad didn't understand. Dr. Thompson said there were going to be twins and Mom had to stay off her feet. But Dad said they would work it out.

"Now, now." Dad's voice was calm as he stood behind Mom's chair, massaging her shoulders. "Everything will be all right."

Chad leaned against the counter staring at the pizza.

"But I *can't* housebreak a puppy now!" Mom insisted. "I can't take care of a puppy when I have to stay off my feet!"

"Mom," Chad groaned, "Fudge is ours already. Dad made a deposit."

Dad gave Chad a warning look. "We'll talk about it tomorrow. Tonight we celebrate! Chad, pour your mother a glass of milk. I'll reheat the pizza." He shook his head as he slid the cooling pizza back into the oven. "Twins! I can't believe it!"

Chad set a large glass of milk in front of Mom. "*I* can housebreak Fudge, Mom. You won't have to do *anything*. I've got a library book that tells how."

Dad gave Chad another look. But Mom put her arm around Chad and pulled him close. "Dad is right, Chad. I'm tired and hungry and excited. We'll talk about it tomorrow." Then she released him and drank the whole glass of milk.

Mom called Grandma Olsen, Uncle Stephen, and her best friends. Dad called Grandpa and Grandma Abernathy in New York. Chad tried to act happy about Mom's news too. When Dad said they should name the babies Abby and Nat if they were girl and boy twins, Chad forced a laugh.

"Abby and Nat Abernathy?" Mom giggled.

When Mom talked about buying two of everything instead of one, Chad said he had to go to the bathroom. He wasn't interested in cribs and strollers and baby clothes. He only wanted Mom to say okay—that he *could* take care of Fudge—that there was nothing to talk about tomorrow.

4

On Friday Mom got ready for work for the last time. She planned to work half a day, have lunch with her bank friends, then come home.

Chad wanted to talk about Fudge at breakfast. He brought all four library books to the table along with his list of things Fudge needed. He flipped open *Dog Training for Kids* to the chapter about housebreaking. "Take your puppy out immediately after feeding," he read aloud. "Praise your puppy when he or she is successful." He looked up from the page. "I can do that."

Dad said, "We'll talk about the puppy this evening, Chad."

Mom put her hand on Chad's shoulder.

"It's not as easy as it sounds in a book. Puppies make a lot of mistakes before they learn." Then she handed Dad his coffee, and they began talking about the twins again.

Chad put the books back in his room. Then he got dressed and went to the Garcias'. It was the last morning he *had* to go. Mom would be home every day from now on.

As soon as he got there, Chad told Tomas, Carmella, Anna, and Mrs. Garcia about the twins. He didn't tell them that Dr. Thompson had said Mom couldn't lift or climb stairs until the babies were born. He didn't tell them that Mom had said she couldn't train a puppy now.

"Twins! How wonderful!" Mrs. Garcia exclaimed, clasping her hands together. "I always wanted twins!"

"Oh, Chad, you're *so* lucky," Carmella said. "Two babies!"

"I'm glad Little Joe isn't twins," Tomas said, laughing.

Chad laughed too and tried not to worry. Last night Dad had said things would work out—they would talk today. But Mom's words stuck in Chad's mind: "How can we manage the puppy *now*?"

It was a warm day, and Mrs. Garcia said

the puppies could play in the fenced back-yard. Carmella and Anna carried a puppy under each arm. Tomas carried out Piggie, Figgie, and Ziggie and set them down by the big maple.

Chad made two trips. He carried Fudge and Bear out last. Fudge was still the smallest puppy, but she didn't let the others get the better of her. On the ground she leaped at Ziggie, chased Napper under the porch, and pounced on Bear when he tried to bite her tail. "That's a girl!" Chad cheered. "Get him good!"

Fudge growled and rolled Bear into the grass.

"Stop her! She's hurting him!" Leslie yelled.

Chad hadn't seen Leslie coming around the house. Now she sailed across the yard and scooped Bear into her arms. "Poor Bear," she said. "Are you hurt?" Then she stomped her foot at Fudge.

"Stop it!" Chad shouted. "They were only playing. Besides, Bear is always picking on Fudge!"

"Come on, Leslie," Tomas said. "Put Bear down and let him play. The puppies won't be together much longer."

"Oh," Leslie said. For a moment she held Bear close. Then she put the puppy back on the ground with the others.

"Mama says the puppies can leave Biggie on Sunday," Carmella said. "Will you take Fudge home right away, Chad?"

"Are you going to buy Bear?" Anna asked Leslie.

Chad wasn't sure how to answer. But Leslie said, "My father is in Ohio this week. When he gets home, he'll give me the money."

"Why don't you give us a deposit?" Tomas asked. "Like Chad's father. Then no one else can buy Bear first."

Leslie sat down on the ground near Bear. "I have ten dollars at home. Maybe eleven." She looked at Tomas. "Will that be enough?" Without waiting for an answer she jumped up, retrieved her skateboard, and was gone.

"Do you think Leslie's father will let her have Bear?" Carmella asked.

"What about her mother?" Tomas said. "*She's* the one who doesn't like dogs. She hasn't even seen the puppies yet."

Carmella sighed. "Chad, you're so lucky. You *know* you get to take Fudge home this weekend. Poor Leslie."

Chad rescued Fudge from Bear again. When he picked her up, she scooted onto his shoulder and began licking his ear. "I'm lucky. I am, I am," he said, hoping it was still true.

Leslie came back with her money tied in a yellow sock. She emptied the sock onto the Garcias' picnic table and announced, "Eleven dollars and fifty cents! Now it's settled! No one else can buy Bear!"

Chad stopped a quarter from rolling off the edge of the table. And Tomas began sorting the money—nickels, dimes, quarters—into neat stacks. There was one five-dollar bill and a lot of pennies.

"I got the five dollars for my birthday," Leslie said. "The rest I saved from my allowance." She left the table to claim Bear.

Carmella and Anna joined her, and soon the girls were laughing together while the puppies played on the grass.

Chad helped Tomas count the money. Tomas swept it all into Little Joe's sandbox pail. "It's all here—eleven dollars and fifty cents!" he called to Leslie. Then he carried the pail into the house.

It was after two o'clock when Mom's car turned the corner at the end of the block.

Chad hurried across the street and waited on the sidewalk while she parked. He wanted to talk to her before Dad came home. He wanted to convince her that he could take care of Fudge. Chad opened the car door when the engine stopped.

"What a morning! What a day!" Mom said as she got out of the car. "The people at the bank insisted on giving me a last-minute surprise party *and* taking me out to lunch. Will you get the packages in back, Chad? I have to lie down before I collapse."

Chad gathered the packages and followed Mom up the walk. "You can lie down every day when we get Fudge," he said. "I'll take care of everything."

Mom gave Chad a weary look. "Chad, I don't want to talk about puppies now. I need to rest." Inside the house she dropped her purse on the sofa and walked down the hall. Chad heard the door of Mom and Dad's bedroom click behind her.

While Mom rested, Chad turned on TV, read a magazine, and ate half a package of raisins. He wished he had not bugged Mom when she was tired. But getting it settled about Fudge was important. Mom had to say okay!

Mom woke up at four o'clock. "I'll need hamburger and four potatoes to start dinner," she said. "Chad, you'll have to get them for me."

The freezer and the potato bin were both in the basement. Chad remembered that Mom should not climb stairs now. He brought up a package of hamburger and four big potatoes.

Then Mom said, "Can you set the table? And take out the garbage? I'll need you to help me with a lot of things from now on." She sat on a kitchen stool wrapping the potatoes in foil.

Chad was used to setting the table, and he took out the garbage whenever Mom asked. So he did both jobs right away. He wanted Mom to be in a good mood when Dad came home and they finally talked about Fudge.

Dad came home at five-thirty, there was more talk about the babies, and Mom told them about her last day at the bank. "They opened a savings account for each baby. Imagine!"

At last dinner was ready and they sat down to eat. Chad buttered his baked potato and began, "Dad, Biggie's puppies will be ready to leave her on Sunday. You told Mr. Garcia we'd take one. You said, 'Put our name on the list' and gave him twenty dollars."

Dad groaned. "Can't we finish dinner before we talk about this?"

"You said, 'We'll take one,'" Chad persisted.

Mom put her hand on Dad's arm. "John, you told Chad we'd talk about it today. I put him off this afternoon—we need to talk about it now." Mom sounded serious and firm.

Dad put down his fork, took a drink of water, and turned to Chad. "I *know* what I said, Chad. At the time your mother and I agreed about getting one of Biggie's puppies. We thought it was a good idea. But now . . ."

"We didn't know about the twins then," Mom interrupted. "We didn't know Dr. Thompson would give me so many rules. Do you understand?"

"No!" Chad hollered. "It's still a good idea!" He jumped up and bumped the table with his arm, and the potato slid off his plate. "We have to take Fudge!" he cried. "We *have* to!"

"We can't," Mom said. She put the potato back on his plate with a hamburger patty. "I know it's a big disappointment, Chad. I want

Fudge too. I even thought of asking Uncle Stephen to housebreak her for us. Then I remembered—Uncle Stephen can't have pets in his apartment."

"We'll get a puppy after the babies are born," Dad promised.

Chad poked at his food. "Fudge will be gone by then. Someone else will have her." He squeezed his eyes shut to keep from crying. Then he said he wasn't hungry and went to his room.

Across the street Biggie was barking. Chad looked out and saw Tomas and Mr. Garcia playing catch. Biggie was trying to get the ball, and the puppies were playing in Little Joe's sandbox.

Chad turned away from the window. "I don't want any other puppy," he sobbed. "I want Fudge."

5

Chad had a plan for keeping Fudge. He thought of it that night—after Mom came into his room to say good night. She sat down on his bed and plumped his pillow, the way she did when he was sick.

"I hate it that you're so unhappy," Mom said. "I hope you are not unhappy about *two* little brothers—or sisters—instead of one."

"It's not the babies' fault," Chad said.

"It isn't anybody's fault," Mom said.

But Chad did blame Mom and Dad for not believing he *could* take care of Fudge on his own. They hadn't even looked at his list. They hadn't given him a chance to tell about his plans for training her.

"Both Baby Abernathys are awake to-night," Mom said. "Do you want to feel them kicking?"

Chad placed his hand on Mom's stomach, and the babies moved *thump, thump a bump* against his palm.

"Do you feel them?" Mom asked.

Chad nodded. He wished he could tell the babies about Fudge. They would like her, he knew. They would want Mom and Dad to change their minds. "Mom," Chad asked, "can't we manage Fudge somehow? I want her so much."

"Things can't always be the way we want them, Chad," Mom said. "I don't like staying off my feet and obeying Dr. Thompson's other rules. I don't like disappointing you after we promised you a puppy." She traced a circle on Chad's back with her finger.

Chad kissed Mom good night, but he didn't give her his best hug. After she left, he lay awake for a long time watching the moonlight make weird shadows in his room. A shadow on the wall looked like Mom rocking a baby in each arm. Another, on the ceiling, looked like Mrs. Garcia holding one of Biggie's puppies—it looked like Fudge.

Chad sat up in bed, still looking up. The shadow on the ceiling gave him an idea. Uncle Stephen couldn't keep Fudge for them, but the Garcias could! Fudge could stay across the street until the babies were born. *He* would feed and care for her every day. *He* would teach her to go outside instead of on the porch newspapers. Fudge wouldn't be any trouble for Mom at all.

Chad wanted to tell Mom and Dad his idea right away. He got up and went to his bedroom door. But the house was dark, except for the night-light in the hall. Mom and Dad had gone to bed. Chad went back to his bedroom and thought about his plan until he fell asleep.

The next day was Saturday. When Chad got up it was nine o'clock, and Mom and Dad were at the kitchen table. Mom was studying paint charts from the hardware store. Dad had already removed everything from the spare room.

"We decided to let you sleep this morning," Mom said.

Dad held up one of the charts. "What do you think, Chad—green for the babies' room? Your mother likes yellow."

Chad looked at the paint samples. He didn't care what color Dad painted the babies' room—as long as it wasn't pink *or* purple. He only wanted to get Mom and Dad to agree to his plan for keeping Fudge.

"Yellow would make the room brighter, sunnier," Mom said.

Chad thought of standing on a chair like Mom to get their attention. Instead he said, "Mom, Dad. I've got some big news." Then he told them his plan. "Can I ask the Garcias, Mom? We can still own Fudge and you won't have to manage a thing!" He waited for Mom and Dad's agreement.

Instead Mom set aside the charts. "This is so hard, John," she told Dad. Then she pulled Chad close like she'd done before. "Chad, we can't take advantage of the Garcias. Don't you see? They've been good neighbors to care for you while I worked."

"We can't ask them to hold Fudge for three months," Dad said.

"They wouldn't be holding her! Fudge would be ours!" Chad insisted. He explained his plan again. "We'd finish paying for her— I've got thirteen dollars in my bank!"

In the end, the answer was no. Chad could

not ask the Garcias to keep Fudge for three months. Once more Dad promised to get another puppy—a Labrador retriever—after the babies were born. Then he left for the paint store.

"We'll have to tell the Garcias we won't be taking Fudge," Mom said. "Do you want me to call Mrs. Garcia?"

"I'll tell them," Chad said. He let the door bang behind him on his way outside.

Everyone was in the Garcias' backyard— Biggie, her puppies, all the Garcias, and Leslie. Leslie wore unmatched sneakers on her feet, the way she did sometimes—one pink, one yellow.

"Chad!" she hollered as he crossed the street. "My father is home from Ohio! And I get to buy Bear!"

"Yay, yay, yay!" Carmella and Anna shouted.

"Great!" Mr. Garcia said happily. "Two of Biggie's puppies get to stay in the neighborhood."

Tomas looked happy too, and Leslie was in the middle of everything, hugging Bear.

Chad couldn't tell them his bad news, not now. He picked Fudge up and pretended to be happy. He told Leslie he was glad she was getting Bear. But when Fudge snuggled against him and pushed her wet nose into his ear, Chad's throat ached. "Fudge, Fudge," he whispered. Then he put her down quick and ran out of the yard before he started crying.

Tomas caught up with him in the alley. "Chad! What's wrong? Did you want Bear, instead of Fudge?"

Chad shook his head. "I *want* Fudge. But I can't have her!" He explained Dr. Thompson's rules for Mom and the babies. He told Tomas he knew he could manage Fudge without Mom's help. He even told about his plan to keep Fudge at Tomas's house until the babies were born. "They both said no!" Chad finished.

"That's a real bummer," Tomas said. He walked with Chad to the end of the alley. When Leslie, Carmella, and Anna ran down the street toward Leslie's, Tomas said, "Let's go back and talk to my mother. Maybe she can do something."

Chad didn't think Mrs. Garcia could do anything. Tomorrow Fudge would be ready to leave Biggie. Mr. Garcia would give back Dad's deposit and Fudge would be sold to someone else. Chad swallowed hard thinking about Fudge living somewhere else—about someone else giving her a new name. What if someone bought Fudge and called her Runty, the way Mr. Garcia did!

Mrs. Garcia was hanging sheets on the clothesline that stretched from the house to the garage. Her mouth was full of clothespins, and she had a wet sheet draped over her shoulder like a cape. Little Joe was playing in his sandbox. Biggie and the puppies were asleep under the maple tree.

"Mama," Tomas said, "Chad needs your help. Tell her, Chad."

Chad spilled it out, all at once. "Dr. Thompson said my mother has to stay off her feet. No lifting, no climbing. She had to quit her job already. We can't take Fudge."

Mrs. Garcia pinned the sheet to the line and took the clothespins out of her mouth. "I understand. Your mother must obey her doctor, Chad. She cannot be troubled with training a puppy now."

"That's not the problem," Chad explained. "I can take care of Fudge myself—I know I can. She wouldn't be any trouble for Mom."

"But his folks said no," Tomas said. He handed his mother a pillowcase from the laundry basket. Mrs. Garcia fastened it to the line and reached for another.

"Mama?" Tomas said.

"I'm thinking, Tomas. I'm thinking." She hung the rest of the laundry before she sat down at the picnic table to rest. Tomas and Chad joined her.

"Maybe you have to *prove* you can take care of a puppy, Chad," she said at last. "Maybe then your parents will change their minds."

"Prove it? How? How can I prove anything if they don't buy Fudge?" Chad asked.

Mrs. Garcia tucked a strand of dark hair behind one ear. She pulled Little Joe out of the sandbox and brushed him off. "Maybe . . ."

Chad and Tomas waited.

"Maybe you could take Fudge on trial."

"Hey!" Tomas hollered. "I told you my mother would think of something!"

But Chad didn't understand. "On trial? Dad got a snow blower on trial last winter. Is that what you mean?"

"Mama, is that what you mean?" Tomas echoed.

Mrs. Garcia nodded. "Something like that. A week—ten days, Chad—to prove you can handle a puppy by yourself. We'd have to ask

Mr. Garcia first, when he gets home. Then we'd speak to your parents."

"Yippee!" Tomas yelled.

Chad gave Mrs. Garcia a quick hug. He was pretty sure Mr. Garcia would agree to the trial. Mr. Garcia wanted Fudge to stay in the neighborhood. Chad didn't know what Mom and Dad would say. Mom might argue that it was too much for Chad. Dad would worry that Mom thought it was too much for Chad. But now, at least, there was a chance of keeping Fudge.

The puppies woke up, Carmella and Anna came back from Leslie's, and Dad hollered for Chad. Chad held Fudge a long moment before starting home. When she squirmed against his chest, he knew he couldn't stand to part with her.

He hurried across Franklin Street feeling hopeful. Then he remembered—Dad had taken the snow blower back at the end of the trial. Mom had said it was too big and too noisy and too expensive. But that would not happen with Fudge.

6

All afternoon Chad watched for Mr. Garcia's truck. Mr. Garcia was helping a friend build a wooden fence, and Mrs. Garcia said it might take all day.

Dad was giving the babies' room a second coat of yellow paint. Chad had helped with the first coat, but it didn't cover. The leaf pattern on the old wallpaper still showed through.

Now Chad stood at the front door, looking out. Mom sat across the living room in front of the big fan. She was knitting something yellow for the babies.

"It seems funny to need two of everything—two sweaters, two caps," Mom said. "I can't get used to the idea." The ball of yarn bounced in her lap as she worked, and the knitting needles clicked like crickets' wings.

Chad had wanted to tell Mom and Dad about Mrs. Garcia's idea. It was hard keeping it to himself. But what if Mr. Garcia got home and *didn't* agree to sell them Fudge on trial?

"Did you knit sweaters and caps for me?" Chad asked.

"Dozens, and I still have them somewhere in the attic. After the babies are born, we can go up and look for them." Mom stopped knitting. "No climbing, lifting, or bending now." She stretched and arched her back, and the ball of yarn bounced to the floor. It unrolled itself to the middle of the room. "Darn! Double darn!" Mom said. She leaned forward, reaching for the yarn.

"No bending, Mom," Chad said. He picked up the ball of yarn, rewound it, and placed it back on her lap.

"This is going to be so hard," Mom groaned suddenly. "Sitting, resting, not being able to go to the attic whenever I choose." She put the knitting aside and pressed her fists to her forehead.

Chad thought Mom was going to cry. So he

moved behind her chair and began rubbing her shoulders. "It's okay. Things will work out." He tried to sound like Dad.

Mom lowered her hands and turned. "You understand, don't you, Chad? You're not a little kid anymore." Her eyes were very green, like the grapes Chad liked from the market. She reached for his hand and squeezed it.

"I'm nine and a half," Chad reminded her. "I'll be ten in January."

Mom laughed and hugged him. It seemed like a good time to ask about taking Fudge on trial. But Dad walked into the room, rubbing his hands on a paint rag. Chad decided to wait for Mr. Garcia.

"Finished. And the room looks great!" Dad said. "How about helping me clean up, Chad?"

After the paint rollers, brushes, and pans were put away, Chad looked across the street again. Mr. Garcia's truck was not in the driveway and it was after four o'clock. How long did it take to build a fence? Chad wondered. He hated waiting, just like Mom.

At five o'clock Chad set the table. Mom sliced tomatoes, onions, carrots, and fresh green beans for a salad. And Dad fried bacon and eggs for sandwiches.

Chad was looking out the kitchen window when the Garcias came up the front walk. Mr. Garcia was carrying Little Joe on his shoulders. Mrs. Garcia walked beside him, with Tomas, Carmella, and Anna close behind. Mr. Garcia had agreed to the trial—Chad knew it!

"Mom! Dad! The Garcias are coming!" he hollered, and rushed outside. Tomas, Carmella, and Anna scrambled onto the porch.

Tomas nudged Chad with his elbow. "My father said *yes!*"

"Shhhh, Tomas," Mrs. Garcia said. "This is between Papa and Chad's parents."

"Is your mama home, Chad?" Mr. Garcia asked. "Your papa too?" He sat Little Joe down on the porch steps and leaned against the railing.

"Mom, Dad!" Chad called. His heart raced as Dad opened the screen door. "Hurry!" he urged. "Mr. Garcia wants to talk to you."

"Hello, Maria. Sergio," Mom said. She sat down on the porch swing, asking Mrs. Garcia to join her.

"What's this about?" Dad asked.

Mrs. Garcia smoothed her dress. "Chad told us you can't take Fudge now, because of the doctor's rules." She patted Mom's arm. "You must do as your doctor says."

"I've quit at the bank already," Mom said.

Chad wished Mrs. Garcia would get to the reason they'd come.

"We're sorry we can't take the puppy," Dad said.

"That's why we've come," Mr. Garcia said, "to make an agreement."

"About Fudge," Tomas blurted.

Dad glanced at Chad. "We made it clear to Chad—his mother cannot manage a puppy now."

"Yes, yes, we know." Mrs. Garcia clapped a hand over Tomas's mouth. "But Chad says he can manage Fudge by himself."

"Mom, I *can*! I *can*, Dad!" Chad insisted.

Mom sighed, and Dad shook his head.

"I, we . . ." Mrs. Garcia continued, taking Mr. Garcia's arm. "We decided to offer you Fudge on trial. One week for Chad to prove whether he can manage or not."

"I can do it, Dad! Mom won't have to help. I can train Fudge myself!"

"What about the gerbil, Chad?" Mom asked. "Remember? You said you would take care of her, then *I* did all the work."

Chad did not want to talk about Gerby. He wished he had taken better care of her. Then Mom wouldn't have given her to Uncle Stephen when she had had her babies.

"I was only seven then. I'm not a little kid anymore." Chad looked straight at Mom.

Tomas, Carmella, and Anna sat quietly on the steps. Mr. Garcia pulled Little Joe off the railing. Dad stood near the swing, watching Mom.

"Caring for a puppy is hard work," Mom went on. "Puppies need a lot of attention. They need to be fed and taken out often. You'd have to clean up mistakes in the house."

Chad held his breath.

"Kathleen . . ." Dad said.

"Biggie's puppies poop on the porch," Anna said, and Tomas poked her.

"We make the agreement?" Mr. Garcia asked. "You take the puppy for one week. If Chad cannot manage, no problem. We'll take her back and sell her with the rest."

"It sounds fair," Dad said, looking at Mom.

"Just so Chad understands," Mom warned. "If he cannot handle Fudge, *without my help*, she goes back."

"Does that mean yes?" Chad asked, and when Mom nodded, he could hardly believe it.

"Yippee! Yippee!" Carmella and Anna hollered.

Tomas leaped from the steps yelling, "Yay! Yay!"

They all circled Chad, including Little Joe—jumping, shouting, shrieking. Chad laughed and shouted too.

Finally Mr. Garcia shook hands with Dad and lifted Little Joe back onto his shoulders. Then he hurried his family down the walk toward home.

"Congratulations on the twins!" Mrs. Garcia called over her shoulder.

Chad sat down on the swing and gave Mom his best hug. "Thanks, Mom. Thanks, thanks, thanks." The words bubbled from his throat like bright balloons.

"I hope we're not making a big mistake," Mom said. "It won't be 'Thanks, Mom,' if we have to give Fudge back."

"We won't! We won't!" Chad said, laughing. Then he saw Leslie rounding the corner on her skateboard. "Leslie!" he shouted without thinking. "I get to bring Fudge home tomorrow." He forgot that Leslie didn't know that he'd almost lost out on Fudge.

"Big news!" Leslie yelled. She sailed right past without stopping. She looked angry.

What now? Chad thought. He couldn't think of anything *he'd* said to make her mad. He'd told her he was happy about Bear. He hadn't made fun of her weird shoes.

"Leslie! Wait up!" Chad hollered, hurrying down the steps. He caught up with Leslie at her front walk. She stood with her skateboard under one arm, the wheels still spinning.

Chad started talking. "It *is* big news, Leslie. First Mom and Dad said we would buy Fudge. Then they said we couldn't because of the babies," he explained. "Now it's settled. Fudge is staying in the neighborhood like Bear!" He didn't tell her about the one week's trial.

"Well, now *I* can't have Bear!" Leslie snapped. "My mother says I can't bring him home because of my sister's allergies!"

"I didn't know your sister had allergies," Chad said.

"Jennifer's allergic to everything!" Leslie yelled, kicking a rock into the gutter. "She's allergic to cats—so we had to get rid of Sneeze. Now I can't have Bear!" Suddenly Leslie burst into tears—tears that plopped down her nose and ran down her cheeks.

Chad had never seen Leslie cry before. He scuffed his heel on the sidewalk. "It's not fair," he said.

"It's rotten, that's what it is!" Leslie shouted. "Rotten rotten rotten!"

"Leslie, stop yelling!" Leslie's mother called from the Pattersons' front doorway. "Come inside if you plan to throw a tantrum!"

Chad watched Leslie march toward the house swinging her skateboard like a bat. What would he do if he had a mother like Mrs. Patterson? he wondered. Or a sister who had allergies? He walked back home feeling sorry for Leslie again, but happy for himself. Fudge *was* coming home tomorrow. Someone else might buy Bear, but not Fudge!

7

Chad wanted to bring Fudge home right away.

"Tomorrow is soon enough," Dad said. "We have to get things ready."

Mom stretched and yawned. They had finished eating and were on the porch again. "We don't have puppy food or a place for her to sleep yet."

"We can borrow some puppy food from the Garcias," Chad said. "And she can sleep with me."

"Tomorrow," Dad said firmly. "And Fudge will sleep by herself until she is housebroken."

Dad was right. Mrs. Garcia was still changing the puppies' newspapers every morning and every night. Chad decided he would read *Dog Training for Kids* again—especially the chapter about housebreaking. He wanted to start off right with Fudge.

But now he wanted to tell Fudge good night and thank Mrs. Garcia for her great idea. Maybe she had good ideas about housebreaking a puppy too. The Garcias had gotten Biggie when she was small.

Tomas was sorting his baseball cards at the picnic table when Chad stepped through the gate. Biggie lay at his feet, and near the sandbox the puppies tumbled in the grass. No one else was in the yard.

As soon as the puppies saw Chad, they came barreling toward him. Chad was ready to scoop up Fudge, but Bear got there first. The big puppy jumped at Chad's legs, barking wildly, until Chad picked him up. Next Ziggie, Fudge, and Napper plowed into Chad's feet.

"Hold it!" Chad exclaimed. "Stop biting my shoes!" He couldn't pick them all up at once, so he sat down on the ground. Immediately Bear leaped from his arms to chase after Fudge. But when she bit his tail, he scrambled back to Chad.

"Poor Bear! Are you hurt?" Chad asked.

"Poor Bear—he has to live with Leslie," Tomas joked.

"Not now," Chad said. "Didn't Leslie tell you? Her sister is allergic to dogs."

"To Bear?" Tomas asked.

"To everything," Chad explained. He pulled Bear into his lap and examined the puppy's tail. Poor Leslie. She loved Bear as much as he loved Fudge. Now someone else would buy Bear and rename him, and Leslie would never see him again. Chad pulled Fudge onto his lap too. "We're lucky, Fudge, you know that?"

Just then Mrs. Garcia called from the porch, "Boys! Bring the puppies inside now! It's getting late!"

Tomas collected his baseball cards, and Chad stood up with Bear and Fudge. He wished Leslie's sister weren't allergic to Bear. He wished both puppies could stay in the neighborhood forever.

"Tomas, let's talk to your mother again," Chad said. "Maybe she can do something about Bear and Leslie."

"I don't know—Mama doesn't know the Pattersons very well," Tomas said. "But I have to tell her about Bear." He scooped Napper up and grabbed Ziggie, too.

Mrs. Garcia was on the porch, changing the puppies' newspapers. "I'll hate to see the puppies go," she said. "But not the mess."

Chad and Tomas held the puppies out of the way while Mrs. Garcia worked. Tomas glanced at Chad and said, "Mama, Leslie can't take Bear."

"Tomas, are you sure?" Mrs. Garcia gathered the soiled newspapers. "I *wondered* why her parents didn't come to see the puppies."

"Leslie's sister is allergic," Chad explained. "She was allergic to Leslie's cat, and now Bear."

Mrs. Garcia sighed. Then she told Tomas and Chad to bring in the rest of the puppies while she got their supper ready. Outside, Chad and Tomas rounded up Piggie, Figgie, Napper, and the others. "I don't think Mama can do anything," Tomas said. Chad didn't think so either.

Mrs. Garcia didn't know how to help Leslie. But she knew a lot about allergies. "My friend Marta is allergic to feathers," she said. "Especially her mother-in-law's parakeet. She has to get allergy shots when they go to St. Louis."

"Leslie's sister could get shots for Bear," Tomas suggested.

Mrs. Garcia went on. "Aunt Jessie is allergic

to cats, but not dogs. She and Uncle Carlos have two short-haired pointers."

"Bear has short hair," Chad said.

The Garcias' automatic yard light went on, and Mrs. Garcia said it was time for Chad to go. Chad picked Fudge up and pressed his face into her fur. "You're coming home tomorrow," he said, and set her down with the others. Then he headed home thinking about Leslie and Bear. Maybe Leslie's sister was not allergic to *short*-haired dogs. If she was, maybe she could get allergy shots like Mrs. Garcia's friend.

At home Dad and Mom were watching TV in the living room. Chad told Mom and Dad about Leslie's problem. "Why did Leslie's father say she could have Bear when she couldn't?" he asked.

"Maybe Leslie's father spoke too soon," Dad said.

"Or doesn't understand about allergies," Mom added.

Chad didn't understand the Pattersons. That night he lay awake, thinking about Leslie. He didn't think Mrs. Patterson would make Jennifer get allergy shots just so Leslie could have Bear.

The next morning Chad got up early and read the chapter about housebreaking. The book said there were two methods—paper training and outside training. If you paper trained your puppy, you were supposed to put him on newspapers to do his job after every meal. Chad didn't think Mom would like having messy newspapers on the floor. When you outside trained your puppy, you were supposed to take your puppy outdoors after every meal. "Choose the spot where you want your puppy to do his job and take him there," the book said. Chad knew he would have to train Fudge to go outside.

Chad put the book away and made a new list, "Things for Fudge." When he heard Mom and Dad getting up, he took his money out of Tyrannosaurus rex and tied it in a sock. Then, at breakfast, he handed the list to Dad.

"Dog bed, red food dish, yellow water bowl, Puppy Bright puppy food," Dad read. "Brown leash, brown collar, and toys. Whew, that's quite an order."

"Fudge can eat out of mixing bowls until we know she is going to stay," Mom said.

Chad frowned. He wanted new dishes for

Fudge. He wanted everything new. Fudge *was* going to stay—for good!

"Chad's old playpen is in the garage," Dad said. "Fudge can have it for her bed. We might need the old baby gate, too. They're both too wrecked for the babies."

"I have money for a *new* collar and *new* leash," Chad said, holding up the sock. "And we *have* to buy puppy food."

"Let's get going, then," Dad said. He put the list in his pocket, hugged Mom, and held the screen door for Chad.

First Dad stopped for gas; then they headed for the pet store in the mall. Chad walked right to the leash-and-collar display. "I want a brown leash and a brown collar," he told the saleswoman. "They're for a Labrador retriever puppy—eight weeks old."

The saleswoman sorted through the collars hanging on the wall. "This size should fit," she said, handing a brown nylon collar to Chad. Then she unhooked a brown nylon leash. The two items came to eight dollars and fifty-four cents, and Chad set his sock on the counter.

"I'll pay for *this*," Dad said as he placed a ten-pound sack of Puppy Bright next to the sock. Then he handed the saleswoman a squeaky toy shaped like a bone and smiled at Chad. "This too. Every puppy needs a special toy."

At home Dad dragged the playpen and the baby gate out of the garage. Chad brushed off the dust, scrubbed them both with soapy water, and rinsed them clean. When they were dry, Dad carried them into the house.

"We'll keep Fudge in the kitchen until she is housebroken," Mom said. "Put the playpen in the corner. Put the gate by the doorway— we can attach it later, and hook it when we want to keep Fudge in."

Chad spread an old blanket on the bottom of the playpen. Dad put the sack of Puppy Bright on the counter. And Mom took two small mixing bowls out of the cupboard.

"*Now* everything is ready," she said. "*Now* you can bring Fudge home, Chad."

Chad banged out of the house, down the sidewalk, and across Franklin Street with his heels flying. The Garcias were in their backyard, eating at the picnic table.

"Come have a hamburger, Chad!" Mr. Garcia called. He waved a catsup bottle in one hand.

"Have some sweet corn!" Carmella said.

Biggie was lying under the table near Little Joe. When Little Joe dropped a piece of hamburger on the ground, Biggie snapped it up. Chad didn't see the puppies anywhere, but he guessed they were inside.

"I've come to get Fudge," Chad said. "Where is she?"

Mr. Garcia laughed. "We put the puppies on the porch when we eat outside—so we can eat in peace."

"We'll be finished soon," Mrs. Garcia added.

Chad watched the Garcias eat and eat. He thought they would never finish. But at last Mr. Garcia pushed back his plate, got up from the table, and started toward the house. "I'll get Fudge!" he called over his shoulder.

In a few minutes he came out of the house with Fudge. He placed her in Chad's arms and everyone crowded close, even Biggie.

"Feed her four times a day—every four hours," Mrs. Garcia said. "She'll be ready to eat again at four."

"Don't let her poop on your porch," Anna advised.

Tomas held Little Joe up, and Little Joe gave Fudge a kiss. "Bye-bye, Fushie," he said.

No one said anything about Fudge being

sold on trial. Chad was halfway across the street when Mrs. Garcia hollered, "Good luck, Chad!"

Chad held Fudge close as she tried to wiggle out of his arms. "We're almost home, Fudge," he said. "We're almost home."

Chad set Fudge down in the middle of the kitchen floor. "Here she is!" he announced. He fitted the brown collar around her neck and said, "Fudge, this is your new home!"

For a moment Fudge stood, looking bewildered. Then she spotted Mom's big toe poking out of her sandal and charged.

"Ouch!" Mom yelped. "That hurt, you little rascal!"

Chad giggled and pulled Fudge out from under the table. Next Fudge spotted the laces on Dad's tennis shoes. Her feet slid every which way as she careened across the vinyl floor.

"We're in for it now!" Dad said, laughing.

Chad sat at the table with Mom, watching

Fudge attack Dad's shoelaces. She grabbed one and shook it fiercely. Then, suddenly, she stopped playing, squatted, and puddled on the kitchen floor.

"Oops," Mom said.

Chad grabbed a handful of paper towels. "She's just excited. She isn't used to us yet."

"You'll have to get rid of the odor, Chad," Dad said. He filled a small bucket with soapy water and handed the bucket and sponge to Chad.

"I don't mind cleaning up," Chad said. He wiped up Fudge's puddle, then scrubbed the spot clean. "She'll learn to go outside soon."

At four o'clock it was time to feed Fudge. Chad put a mixing bowl on the counter. Then he opened the package of Puppy Bright. Fudge understood the rattle meant *food,* and she sat with her tail thumping the floor.

"Read the directions first," Mom said.

"I *know* how, Mom," Chad said. "Three cups of puppy meal—one cup of warm water." He measured two cups into the bowl before he realized that three cups was enough for *three* puppies. He had goofed already.

"Maybe one cup for Fudge," Dad suggested. "And one-third cup of water." He

showed Chad how to use Mom's measuring cup while Fudge barked at their feet.

Chad mixed the food, and Dad filled the other bowl with cool water. Then they stood back to watch Fudge eat.

"What a messy eater." Mom laughed. "She's even got her ears in the act."

Fudge snorted like a pig as she went after her meal.

"She's messy *and* noisy," Dad said.

When Fudge finished eating, Chad cleaned her off with a wet paper towel. Then he snapped the new leash onto her collar. "Take your puppy out after every meal," the library book said. Chad walked Fudge to the back door, outside, and across the yard to the garage.

"Okay, Fudge, do your job," Chad said.

Fudge sniffed the grass, the garbage cans, and the lilac bush at the corner of the garage. Then she circled the area, sniffing everything else.

"Okay, Fudge, do your job now," Chad repeated.

At last Fudge found a spot behind the garage where she squatted and puddled on the grass. Then she did her big job by the garbage cans.

"Good girl! Good dog!" Chad praised her —the way the book said to do when your puppy was successful. Then he hugged Fudge and hurried her back to the house. Mom and Dad would be impressed—Fudge was almost housebroken already.

"She did it!" Chad said. "She went outside!"

Both Mom and Dad praised Fudge too, and Dad unwrapped the puppy toy shaped like a bone. But instead of playing with it, Fudge ran under the table.

"What's wrong? Don't you like your toy?" Dad asked.

"Maybe she's afraid of it," Mom said.

But Fudge wasn't afraid of the toy. Before Chad could stop her, Fudge did another job right by Mom's feet.

"Pheweee!" Dad said.

Chad cleaned up the mess, and Fudge got in the way. When he scrubbed the floor, she attacked the sponge. Mom laughed hard, and Dad laughed too. Chad was glad they weren't angry about the mess and that they didn't remind him Fudge was just on trial.

When it was time to take Fudge out again,

Chad made sure he kept her out long enough to finish her job. He remembered to praise her too. "Good Fudge! Good, good dog!" he said, patting her heartily.

At nine-thirty Mom said, "Time for bed."

Chad had taken Fudge out for the last time. Now she and Chad were playing with an old sock Dad had tied into a knot. Chad tossed the sock and said, "Get it, Fudge!" When Fudge dropped the sock back in Chad's lap, Dad said she was acting like a retriever already.

"Aw, Mom. We're having fun. It's too early to go to bed," Chad complained.

"Fudge needs her rest. So do you," Mom insisted. "It's been a hectic day."

Chad didn't argue. He picked Fudge up and placed her in the playpen. "This is your new bed, Fudge—until you're housebroken. Then you can sleep with me."

But Fudge was not ready to settle down. She jumped at the side of the pen. She grabbed a corner of the blanket and shook it hard.

"Lie down, Fudge," Dad said.

"She'll quiet down when we turn out the light," Mom said.

Chad lingered by the playpen—he didn't want to leave Fudge yet.

"Good night, Fudge," Dad said as he urged Chad out of the kitchen. Immediately Fudge began to whine.

"Fudge must stay in the playpen at night," Mom said, and turned off the light.

Fudge's cries followed them to the living room, where Dad picked up a book and Mom sat down to knit. Chad stood in the hallway, listening, as the cries got louder.

"Go to bed, Chad," Mom said firmly.

"Maybe she's hurt or something. Maybe her paw is caught."

Dad put down his book. "Maybe Fudge misses Biggie and the other puppies," he said. "But we'll check."

Fudge's paw was not caught. The moment Mom turned on the kitchen light, she raced around the playpen, barking happily.

"You're supposed to go to sleep now," Chad said.

"She's not used to sleeping alone," Mom said. "Maybe a hot-water bottle will help." She put the teakettle on, and Dad got the hot-water bottle from the hall closet.

When the hot-water bottle was ready, Dad put it under Fudge's blanket.

"Go to sleep, Fudge," Chad said. He leaned

over the side of the playpen to pet her one last time. Then they all left the kitchen again.

Chad hoped the warmth of the hot-water bottle would comfort Fudge. But even in his bedroom he could hear the *yip yip yip*ping from the kitchen. Fudge's cries sounded so sorrowful—like the wind when it sighed around the willow tree in the backyard.

Dad came in and told Chad not to worry. "Fudge is unhappy, but we can't give in to her, Chad. It will only take a few nights before she learns to sleep alone."

After Dad left, Chad covered his head with his pillow, but he could still hear Fudge crying. He knew she was lonely and maybe afraid of the dark. He waited until Mom and Dad went to bed—then he tiptoed through the darkened house.

When he reached the kitchen, Fudge barked.

"Shhhh! Quiet," Chad whispered as he crossed the room. Then he reached over the side of the playpen and lifted Fudge out. "It's all right. There's nothing to be afraid of," Chad whispered. "I know you miss Biggie and the other puppies." Fudge snuggled close, nuzzling Chad's neck.

The sudden glare of the kitchen light startled Chad. He looked up and saw Dad standing in the doorway. "Put Fudge back in the playpen, Chad, and go back to bed," he said. "Fudge will be all right."

Chad obeyed. He put Fudge on her blanket and followed Dad back to his room. But he didn't fall asleep. Fudge's cries kept him awake for a long time.

In the morning Chad got up while Mom and Dad were still asleep and hurried into the kitchen. "Time to go out, Fudge," he said, lifting her out of the playpen. But it wasn't soon enough. He was attaching Fudge's leash to her collar when she puddled by the door. He was scrubbing the floor when Dad came in.

"I'm in a hurry, Chad. Don't wake your mother, and good luck with Fudge," he said. He gulped a glass of orange juice, grabbed his newspaper, and was gone.

Chad knew that Fudge's crying had kept Mom awake last night, too. He fed Fudge, trying not to make any noise. Then he took her out.

Across the street Tomas was pitching his baseball against the Garcias' garage. The ball made a loud smacking noise when it hit the wall.

"Quiet, Tomas!" Chad called. "My mother is still asleep!" He waited until Fudge did her job, then crossed the street.

"Hey, Fudge! How're you doing?" Tomas said. He scruffed Fudge about the ears and scratched her neck.

"Fudge cried all night—that's why my mother is still asleep," Chad explained.

"I'll bet she misses the other puppies," Tomas said. "But they'll *all* be gone soon. Friends of my parents' want three of the puppies, and the ad will be in the paper tonight."

Just then Chad heard Leslie's skateboard. And soon she turned the corner, looking weirder than ever. She was wearing one of her father's golfing hats turned backward. Chad wondered if she would go right by without stopping. If she stopped, he wondered if he should say anything about Bear.

"Good morning, Chad! Good morning, Tomas!" Leslie called as she sailed toward them. At the Garcias' gate she screeched to a stop, just missing Fudge. "Oh, Fudge," she cooed. "You look so cute with your *brown* collar and your *brown* leash."

Fudge jumped, leaped, and wiggled at Leslie's feet, and Leslie knelt down to hug her.

Chad watched, feeling uncomfortable.

Tomas glanced at him and said, "Chad told us about your sister's allergies, Leslie. I'm sorry you can't have Bear."

Leslie looked up, still petting Fudge—her eyes looked blue and cold. "It doesn't matter, Tomas. Bear is too big anyway, and besides, my mother says male dogs wet on the furniture." Then she stood up, straightened her cap, and pushed off down the sidewalk. "See you!" she called without looking back.

On Monday Fudge only made three mistakes in the house all day, and two were near the back door. "She's trying to tell me when she needs to go out," Chad said at dinner.

"I'm proud of you both," Dad said. "And I'm glad we agreed to give you a chance with Fudge." In the playpen, Fudge chewed on her squeaky toy, making it squeal and wheeze.

"Now if she would just stop crying at night," Mom said.

Chad knew what Mom meant. Last night he had heard Fudge crying with his bedroom door closed *and* his pillow over his head. He wondered how long it would take before she was housebroken and could sleep with him.

After dinner Chad took Fudge for a long walk around the neighborhood. Dad said exercise helped a person sleep soundly. Maybe it would work with puppies, too.

In the middle of the block Mr. Beech was trimming his front hedge. Fudge barked as the clippers snipped branches to the ground. "That's a right brave dog you've got, Chad!" Mr. Beech called.

"Hey, Fudge!" Chad laughed, patting Fudge's rear. "You're brave, all right."

Two doors down Mrs. Johnson was sweeping her sidewalk. Fudge charged at her broom. "That's one spunky puppy!" she said, laughing.

"Spunky and smart!" Chad said.

Chad was leading Fudge home when he saw a gray car turn the corner and park in front of the Garcias'. He watched as a man and two boys got out and went inside. "They're answering the ad," Chad told Fudge. Then he waited until they came out again. The man was carrying one of Biggie's puppies. Chad wanted to cross the street and ask Tomas which one, but Dad called him home.

That night Mom refilled the hot-water bottle, and Dad put an alarm clock in with Fudge.

"Mike Allen at the shop said the ticking reminds puppies of their mother's heartbeat," Dad said.

"I hope Fudge thinks the clock sounds like Biggie," Mom said. She was ready to turn off the light when Chad thought of something else.

"Wait!" he said. He ran to his room and pulled his old stuffed dog from the closet. Wolfie was brown and still fuzzy in spots, and had slept with Chad when he was small.

Chad laid Wolfie next to the clock. "Go to sleep, Fudge. Wolfie will keep you safe."

But Fudge still cried all night. And the next morning Dad got up late again. Mom stayed in bed, and Fudge did a big job by the door before Chad could get her out.

Take Fudge out, feed her at eight, take her out again—Chad did everything in order. Mom was still asleep when he finished, so he turned on the TV.

He took Fudge out of the playpen so she wouldn't bark. He held her on his lap until she got restless. Then he put her in the kitchen and closed the baby gate. "The program will be over soon. Then I'll play with you," he said.

But when Mom got up, she discovered two

puddles on the floor—one in front of the re-frigerator and the other next to the door. Fudge had dragged Mom's knitting off a kitchen chair too.

"You are supposed to put Fudge in the playpen when you're not watching her!" Mom scolded. "You are supposed to take her *outside* when she needs to go."

Chad tried to explain, but Mom wouldn't listen. "You said you could manage by your-self, Chad. But this is just the way it was with Gerby."

Chad put Fudge in the playpen while he soaked up both puddles and scrubbed the floor. He helped Mom untangle the yarn, too, but he thought she should put her knitting away at night. When he was finished, he took Fudge out on the porch.

"I *am* managing," he told Fudge. "And it's *not* like it was with Gerby. I don't forget to feed *you* and I clean up your mistakes right away." Fudge lay across Chad's knee, looking innocent. She barked when she saw Tomas coming up the walk.

"We sold Ziggie and Napper last night," Tomas said. "Someone bought Piggie this morning."

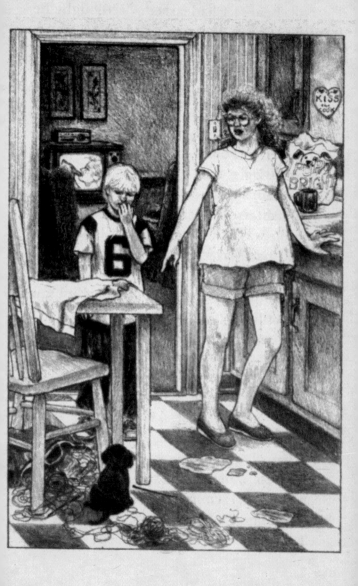

"Not Bear?" Chad asked. "I thought he would be the *first* to go."

Tomas shrugged. "My father decided to give Bear to Aunt Jessie and Uncle Carlos. They're coming from Michigan tonight."

"Don't they have two dogs already?" Chad asked.

"Pointers," Tomas said. "But they want a dog like Biggie, too."

A car horn honked, and Chad turned to see the Pattersons' station wagon go by. Mrs. Patterson was at the wheel, with Leslie next to her. Chad waved, but he didn't see Leslie wave back.

"Guess what," Tomas said. "Last night I saw Leslie in our alley, watching."

"Watching what?" Chad asked.

"Watching the people come for puppies," Tomas said.

Chad pulled Fudge away from the steps. He could picture Leslie skulking in the alley. He could see her scowling and pushing back her bangs, hoping no one would buy Bear.

"She was watching to see if anyone took Bear, I'll bet," Tomas said. "She still wants him, no matter what she says."

Chad grabbed Fudge before she tumbled

off the porch. He had hoped that Leslie would still get Bear, but now Bear would be going to live in Michigan—with pointers.

Mom called Chad inside when Tomas left. "I need some things from the basement," she said. She wanted a jar of peaches and a package of frozen spaghetti for lunch.

Chad put Fudge in the playpen and went downstairs. When he came up, Mom said, "I think taking care of a puppy might be too much for a nine-year-old."

"I'm nine and a half," Chad said. "I'll be ten in . . ."

"January," Mom interrupted. "I know. But being responsible for a puppy is difficult even for an adult. I remember my mother cleaning up after one puppy we had—I don't think it ever got housebroken."

"Fudge is different," Chad said. He leaned over the edge of the playpen and grabbed at her tail. "She is smart and brave and a quick learner. Aren't you, Fudge?"

Mom shrugged. "We got off on the wrong foot this morning, Chad. Let's start over." Then she gave him *her* biggest hug. Chad stretched his arms around Mom's middle as far as they would go. He felt the Baby Abernathys *thump* *bump*ing and wondered if they knew he was out there too.

Mom fixed lunch for Chad and herself, and Chad fixed lunch for Fudge. Then he took Fudge out. When he came in, Mom was hanging up the phone. "I asked Uncle Stephen to dinner," she said. "He hasn't met Fudge yet, and we'll have a cookout."

"Yay!" Chad yelled. He liked Uncle Stephen. Uncle Stephen called him "Old Sport" and saved unusual postage stamps for him. Uncle Stephen had found homes for all of Gerby's babies, and Gerby still lived at the school where Uncle Stephen taught eighth grade. Uncle Stephen would love Fudge. "That's one fine dog, Old Sport," he would say.

At six o'clock Chad waited on the porch steps. Fudge was chasing a beetle in the grass. In the backyard everything was ready. The picnic table was set, and Dad was cooking hamburgers on the grill.

When Uncle Stephen arrived, he jumped up onto the porch and scooped Fudge into his arms. "So this is the mighty Fudge!" he said. Chad laughed when Fudge nipped Uncle Stephen's ear.

Uncle Stephen had a ball for Fudge in his

pocket and a watermelon in his car for the cookout. "We can have a seed-spitting contest later," he said.

Chad liked eating outside. He liked the charcoal smells and eating off paper plates. It didn't matter if you spilled anything. He liked it best when Uncle Stephen joined them.

"Remember Casey?" Uncle Stephen asked Mom while they were eating. "He was the *greatest* dog in the world!"

"Fudge will be greater!" Chad insisted. Under the table Fudge lay at Chad's feet, chewing on her new ball.

Mom laughed. "I remember your pet chicken, Stephen. His name was Dracula, and he attacked feet—*my* feet."

Just then Fudge attacked Chad's feet, and everyone laughed. It was fun when they were all together—and now Fudge was part of the family too.

Dad won the seed-spitting contest. Mom spit a seed into the vegetable garden. Chad and Uncle Stephen both spit seeds into Mom's roses. But Dad spit a seed that hit the garage door with a *ping*.

"Say, Old Sport, I almost forgot," Uncle Stephen said. He pulled two tickets out of his billfold. "The circus is in the city. How about going with me tomorrow?"

"The circus! Tomorrow?" Chad stared at the orange tickets.

"Elephants! Clowns! Wild animals!" Uncle Stephen announced. "Popcorn and peanuts!"

"It's pretty short notice, Stephen," Mom said.

Uncle Stephen shrugged. "I just got the tickets this morning—from a friend who couldn't use them."

Mom sighed, and Dad said, "It's like this, Stephen . . ." and explained about Dr. Thompson's rules for Mom and how the Garcias had let them take Fudge on trial. "Chad is responsible for Fudge."

"Maybe Chad can go on Saturday, when John is home," Mom said.

"The tickets are for tomorrow," Uncle Stephen said. "It's the last day."

Dad and Mom and Uncle Stephen talked and talked, but in the end Chad couldn't go. There was no one else to take care of Fudge.

"Chad understood the terms when we allowed him to take Fudge," Mom said.

Chad sat at the picnic table, poking at a watermelon rind. He wanted to go to the circus. He wanted to see the elephants, clowns, and wild animals and eat popcorn and peanuts, too. "Dad, can't you take a day off?" Chad asked. "Like you did when Grandma Olsen came last Christmas?"

"Not at inventory time, Chad. And not for a circus." Dad doused the grill and carried the charcoal back to the garage. Uncle Stephen picked up the trash and helped Mom carry the rest of the things inside.

"Chad! Bring Fudge inside now!" Mom called from the back door.

"In a minute!" Chad answered. He picked up Fudge's ball and sat down on the grass. "It isn't fair," he said when Fudge scrambled onto his lap. "Why does the circus have to come when I can't go?"

For a minute Fudge nosed Chad's knee, looking for the ball. Then she climbed into his lap and lay quietly—as if she knew he was unhappy. Chad held her close, feeling her heartbeat against him, before he went inside.

That night Chad was still awake when Mom came in to say good night. "Mom," Chad asked, "when will Fudge be old enough to stay by herself?"

Mom sat down on the side of the bed and plumped his pillow. "It's only been two days, Chad. If things work out, Fudge will be housebroken in a few weeks."

"But not by tomorrow," Chad said.

"No," Mom said. "Not in time for the circus."

10

Chad woke up thinking about the circus. Uncle Stephen had made it sound exciting and wonderful—clowns and wild animals in person. Chad had seen circus acts on TV, but it wasn't the same.

Dad stopped in the doorway, putting on his jacket. "Time to get up, Chad," he said. "We're running late again."

Chad hurried into his own clothes. Last night Fudge had cried so loudly that Dad had finally closed the kitchen door. Even then Chad had heard her faint *yip, yip, yip*ping. Lately she'd started howling, too. Dad joked that it was the full moon—all animals felt more restless then. Mom said the babies were more restless too. "Kicking up a storm," she said. Lately Chad felt and *saw* the babies *thump bump*ing more every day.

This morning Mom was in the kitchen eating breakfast. Dad had left for work already, and Fudge was jumping at the sides of the playpen.

"Poor Fudge," Mom said. "She doesn't understand why *I* can't take her out."

Chad lifted Fudge out of the pen and accepted her wet morning kisses. "Poor Fudge," Chad giggled as she mopped his face. As soon as he put her down, she trotted to the door. "At least she waits now," Chad said. "She hasn't puddled on the floor in two mornings."

"Now, if she'd just stop howling," Mom said.

Chad didn't think Fudge would stop until she could sleep with him at night.

Outside, Chad led Fudge behind the garage and waited while she did her usual sniffing. Sometimes she took a long time to find the right spot. While he waited, Chad wondered if Uncle Stephen would take anyone else to the circus or just give the tickets away.

Fudge sniffed grass, bushes, and garbage cans. "Good girl, do your job now," Chad urged.

Across the street the Garcias' back door banged, and Chad looked to see if Tomas had come outside to pitch balls. But no one was in the yard.

Mr. Garcia's truck was in the driveway—next to a camper van. The van was large and white, with a desert scene painted on the side. Chad had forgotten that the Garcias' Aunt Jessie and Uncle Carlos were coming for Bear. He had forgotten about the rest of Biggie's puppies, too. How many had been sold last night? he wondered.

Suddenly Chad had an idea—a great idea like Mrs. Garcia's. *Tomas could take care of Fudge for the day!* "Hey, Fudge," Chad said. "You can play with your brothers and sisters and I can go to the circus!" Fudge pounced on an ant near the garbage cans.

As soon as Fudge found her spot and finished, Chad hurried her down the sidewalk and across Franklin Street.

Tomas answered his knock at the Garcias' back door. He was still in his pajamas and was eating a banana. Before Chad could tell Tomas why he'd come, Tomas whooped, "Chad! Guess what! Aunt Jessie and Uncle Carlos are here with their camper! We're all going to

Silver Lake for the day—even Biggie and the puppies!"

Biggie pushed past Chad into the yard, and two puppies followed—Figgie and Bear. All three welcomed Fudge by barking and wagging their tails. Bear nosed Fudge into the bushes.

Chad's heart sank. He couldn't ask Tomas to watch Fudge now. "I thought they were coming to get Bear," he said.

"They're on vacation—so we're going to Silver Lake," Tomas explained. "Hey! Why don't you come along?"

Chad shook his head. "Uncle Stephen asked me to go to the circus. I just came over to see how many puppies were gone."

"Only Figgie and Bear are left," Tomas said. "And last night Leslie was watching again. She pretended she was just walking by, but she wasn't."

Mrs. Garcia called Tomas to get dressed, and Chad carried Fudge out of the yard. She didn't want to leave Biggie and her brothers yet and wriggled in his arms.

Chad had to jump back to keep from colliding with Leslie on the sidewalk. She came out of the alley at full speed. "Look out!" she yelled, and swerved onto the tree bank.

"What are you doing out this early?" Chad asked.

"It's a free country," Leslie said. Then she reached out and roughed Fudge's ears. She looked angry, but her face softened as Fudge pushed against her hand.

Chad didn't tell Leslie that Bear was going to live in Michigan soon. Instead, watching her with Fudge, he got another idea. Why couldn't *Leslie* watch Fudge while he went to the circus? She could keep Fudge outside, so her sister wouldn't sneeze. She could feed Fudge outside, so there wouldn't be any messes to clean up.

He began, "My uncle asked me to go to the circus today."

"My father took me to the circus *last* summer," Leslie said.

Chad blurted it out. "Can you watch Fudge so I can go?"

Leslie blinked, brushed back her bangs, and scooted Fudge onto her shoulder.

"You could keep Fudge outdoors. I'll bring her food and dishes. We'll be home early."

"I don't know. I have things to do," Leslie said. Then Fudge snuffed her nose into Leslie's hair, making her laugh. "Okay, I'll do it—but just this once."

Chad raced home with Fudge and banged into the kitchen. "I get to go to the circus!" he yelled. "Leslie said she'd watch Fudge!"

"Hold on," Mom said. "First we have to make sure Uncle Stephen still has the tickets. Then I have to check with Leslie's mother."

Chad waited while Mom made the calls. "It's all set," she said at last. "Stephen will pick you up at eleven. Leslie will pick up Fudge at ten-forty-five."

Chad had everything ready at ten-thirty. The mixing bowls, a supply of Puppy Bright, and Fudge's toys—ball, sock, and squeaky toy—were in a shopping bag. At ten-forty-five Chad handed the bag and Fudge's leash to Leslie. "Don't let her run into the street," he said. "Mix her food with warm water."

"I can take care of Fudge," Leslie said. She walked down the sidewalk carrying the shopping bag in one hand and dragging Fudge along with the other.

Chad wasn't sure he wanted to leave Fudge with Leslie. He wished the Garcias weren't going to Silver Lake. "See you later, Fudge!" Chad called after them. Fudge trotted right along with Leslie, not looking back.

Chad was still watching when Uncle Stephen honked at the curb. "Let's go, Old Sport!" he called. Chad waited until Leslie and Fudge turned the corner; then he climbed into the car.

It took an hour to drive into the city. It took half an hour to park and walk to the stadium. All the time Chad thought about Fudge. He tried to think about the circus. Monkeys on swings. Clowns diving into bathtubs. But he kept wondering—would Leslie remember to feed Fudge at noon? Would she remember to give Fudge water?

Their seats were halfway up in the stadium. Uncle Stephen bought popcorn and a program for Chad. Soon the circus began. It was a long circus. The program said it was the biggest show on earth, and Chad believed it. There were thirty-two elephants. There were dozens of clowns. Chad liked the one with the big flat feet best.

But the circus went on and on. There was even an intermission. What was Fudge doing all this time? Chad wondered. Was Leslie watching her so she didn't run off? He ate popcorn, peanuts, and a hot dog. He read the program—there were fourteen acts in all.

The circus lasted three hours. Then it took a half hour to get out of the parking lot, and the expressways were jammed.

"Can't we go any faster?" Chad asked. Fudge would think he had left her with Leslie for good.

"Not unless we sprout wings," Uncle Stephen joked.

It was after five-thirty when they finally got home. "I've got to go after Fudge," Chad said as he bounded out of the car.

Leslie was sitting on her front steps. Fudge was not hurt or lost—she was asleep on the top step. Chad raced up the sidewalk and lifted her into his arms. "Thanks, Leslie," he said, pressing Fudge against him.

Leslie shrugged, and Fudge woke up. At once she greeted Chad with sloppy kisses. "Hey, Fudge, did you miss me?" Chad asked.

"She ate at twelve and four," Leslie said. "She did a big job in Mr. Beech's bushes. And when I had to go to the bathroom, Jennifer watched her." Leslie narrowed her eyes. "*And* Jennifer didn't sneeze *and* her eyes didn't puff up either."

Chad blinked. "She's not allergic to Fudge?"

"Who knows?" Leslie said, jumping up. "I almost forgot—don't leave yet." She ran into the house while Chad waited with Fudge.

In a few minutes Leslie returned with a piece of paper and handed it to Chad. It was a bill. At the top Leslie had printed "Leslie's Dog-Sitting Service" in purple. Below she had listed two amounts in pink.

Dog-sitting—50¢ an hour—$3.00
One tennis shoe—yellow—$1.00

Chad stared at the paper. Leslie had given him a bill for four dollars. "You didn't say anything about charging," Chad said. "And what's the dollar for—a *tennis* shoe?"

"*You* didn't ask if I charged for keeping dogs." Leslie snorted. "And Fudge chewed my shoe. It was old, but it was still good."

"I'll pay you tomorrow," Chad said. Then he led Fudge home, muttering to himself, "Some friend."

11

The Garcias were not back from Silver Lake when Chad took Fudge in for the night. He'd watched for the white van until dark. He wanted to tell Tomas about the circus. But mostly he wanted to tell him about Leslie charging him for taking care of Fudge.

Mom said paying Leslie for dog-sitting was fair. People paid for baby-sitting all the time. Dad agreed, but said that Leslie was responsible for Fudge chewing her shoe.

At bedtime Chad counted the money in his bank and set aside *three* dollars for Leslie. Tyrannosaurus rex was almost empty. He had planned on buying Fudge new dishes, but he couldn't now.

The next morning Fudge trotted right to the back door as soon as Chad took her out of the playpen. "Good dog!" Chad said, and snapped on her leash. When he brought Fudge back inside, he reminded Mom, "Fudge's record is three mornings in a row."

Mom reminded Chad that Fudge had puddled on the floor the night before—when Chad had brought her home from Leslie's.

"She was excited and happy to be home," Chad said, defending her. "Besides, she's only been here four days."

Mom shrugged. "I keep remembering that one dog we had—it was weeks before he stopped puddling. It drove your grandmother nuts."

Chad was feeding Fudge when Tomas, Carmella, and Anna came to the back door. "How was the circus?" Tomas asked.

"Great!" Chad said. He wished he'd enjoyed it more and hadn't worried so much about Fudge. But he showed them the program. "There were lions and elephants and acrobats—fourteen acts in all."

"The lake was crowded," Tomas said.

"Little Joe threw up and Aunt Jessie got sunburned," Carmella said. "And Figgie pooped in the van."

"I wish *we'd* gone to the circus," Anna said.

"Why don't you put on your own circus?" Mom said. "That's what Chad's uncle and I did when we were your age."

Anna jumped up and down. "I want to be a clown."

"I'll be the wild-animal trainer!" Tomas said.

Chad and Tomas and the girls planned their circus while Fudge pulled on their shoelaces and pant legs and gave slurpy kisses. Mom reminded Chad that Fudge had not been out since eating.

"You can do your planning outside," she said. "I need to take my vitamins and lie down awhile. Just let me know when the show begins."

Outside, Tomas waited with Chad while Fudge sniffed in circles and finally did her job. Carmella and Anna ran to tell Leslie about the circus.

While they were gone, Chad told Tomas about Leslie's dog-sitting bill. "I'll pay for the dog-sitting but not for the shoe," he said. He was about to tell Tomas about Jennifer—that her eyes didn't puff up around Fudge and that maybe she *wasn't* allergic to Labrador retrievers.

But just then Carmella and Anna returned

with Leslie. They all decided to hold the circus in the Garcias' backyard. Carmella said their mother would serve lemonade and cookies.

Leslie wanted to be the tightrope walker. "I'll walk on the edge of the sandbox without falling off," she said. "I'll walk carrying a man-eating tiger on my shoulder—Bear!"

Tomas gave Chad a worried look.

"I'll be a clown, like Anna," Chad said. "I'll wear Dad's shoes and stand on my head!"

Everyone had ideas. Figgie and Fudge would be monkeys. Carmella would hang by her feet from the old swing. Biggie would be an elephant, with Little Joe riding on her back.

At noon Mom called Chad in for lunch.

"Two o'clock!" Chad hollered as he led Fudge back to the house. "Tell everyone! That's when the Franklin Street Circus begins!"

"And don't forget the four dollars you owe me!" Leslie called after him.

"*Three!*" Chad yelled back.

Chad ate lunch, fed Fudge, and took her out to the garbage cans. While Fudge did her sniffing, Chad practiced headstands. Standing on your head was hard enough without

106

a puppy joining in. Fudge leaped at Chad's hands, elbows, ears, and hair.

"Oh, Fudge!" Chad laughed as he tumbled to the ground. "I give up!" He grabbed her as she leaped onto his stomach, and wrestled her into a hug.

For the circus Chad dug a pair of Dad's old shoes out of the hall closet. Dad's size twelves were like boats on Chad's feet. "Mom, what else can I wear?" Chad asked. "I'm supposed to be a clown."

"You can wear one of my dresses, if you like. They don't fit me right now," Mom said.

Chad giggled. "Oh, Mom."

In the attic Chad found an old pair of Army pants for himself and an old Army hat for Fudge. She chewed on the brim when Chad tried to put it on her head.

All the kids met at the Garcias' after lunch. Tomas was dressed in long underwear and bathing trunks and carried a flyswatter for a whip. Anna had decided to be an acrobat instead of a clown. She and Carmella wore their bathing suits, with dish towels for capes.

No one knew exactly what to do. By two o'clock Mr. Beech and Mrs. Johnson were seated at the picnic table with Aunt Jessie and

Uncle Carlos. Mrs. Garcia had settled Mom in a folding chair and was sitting on the back steps with other neighbors.

The driveway was the wild-animal ring. The sandbox was the high-wire arena. Chad stood on his head. Carmella hung from the swing by her knees. Anna, Tomas, and Little Joe all marched around getting in each other's way.

"Yay! Yay!" Uncle Carlos cheered when Tomas got Biggie to roll over twice by feeding her chocolate chip cookies.

Mom laughed when Chad stood on his head. Fudge licked his nose, and one of Dad's shoes fell off. Everyone laughed at Little Joe trying to stay on Biggie's back when Biggie kept sitting down.

Leslie's mother didn't come. She had to take Jennifer to a swimming party and pick up Mr. Patterson at the airport. But Leslie put on a show just the same. She waited until the rest of the kids had finished. Then she stood in the middle of the yard and announced, "Ta-da! The great Leslie is about to perform!"

Tomas and Chad exchanged glances. Leslie looked weird. She wore a pink leotard from her dancing class, with a purple bathing suit over it and a man's black cap crammed on her head.

"Ta-da!" Leslie said again. Then she picked up Bear. She had wrapped a yellow scarf around his neck. She had tied a pink ribbon around his tail. Now she lifted him onto her shoulder and stepped onto the rim of the sandbox. She walked around the edge as if she were on a high wire a hundred feet off the ground.

Aunt Jessie clapped and clapped. Uncle Carlos and Mr. Beech yelled, "Bravo!" Chad saw Mom clapping too. She hadn't clapped for his act—she had laughed when the shoe had clunked him on the head on the way down.

Afterward Aunt Jessie helped Mrs. Garcia serve the refreshments. "You and Bear were wonderful," she told Leslie as she offered the tray of lemonade and cookies. "We're so happy Bear is going home with us."

Chad was sitting on the grass nearby. He saw Leslie's face darken and her mouth begin to quiver.

"You're buying Bear?" Leslie said.

"Didn't you know?" Aunt Jessie said. "We're taking him back to Michigan tomorrow."

Chad waited for Leslie to cry, or yell, or throw a tantrum. But she didn't. She helped herself to a handful of cookies and a glass of lemonade. "I've never been to Michigan," she said. "But my father has—he's been everywhere." Then she walked across the yard and sat down on the grass.

"Well, your circus was a success," Mom said. "I wish Stephen and Dad could have been here." Then she giggled. "You were so funny, Chad, kicking the shoe onto your own head."

Chad helped the Garcias clean up, then took Fudge home. He watched TV while Mom rested in her room and Fudge snoozed in her playpen. But he couldn't forget the look on Leslie's face. She had still expected to buy Bear—somehow.

Dad came home with a Frisbee for Fudge. It said "Abernathy Electrical Contractors" on one side. "We might as well start training *our* champion," he said.

Fudge had the Frisbee in her mouth when Tomas raced across the street. "Chad! Have you seen Bear?" he shouted. "He's missing!"

Soon the whole neighborhood was looking for Bear. "He disappeared around dinnertime," Mrs. Garcia said. "One minute he was in the backyard with Biggie and Figgie—the next minute he was gone!"

At once Chad thought of Leslie. But right then Leslie came charging into the yard looking upset. "Bear is lost? He can't be!" she hollered. "We've got to find him!"

Mr. Beech, Dad, Uncle Carlos, and all the Garcias looked for Bear. Neighbors up, down, and around the block joined in the search—including Leslie's father. Chad put Fudge on the Garcias' porch with Figgie. Then he and Tomas took Biggie to find Bear.

"Find your puppy, Biggie," Chad urged. "Find Bear!"

They looked under bushes, behind the garage, and even under the porch steps with Biggie. But no Bear.

Anna started crying. "It's getting dark. Bear isn't used to the dark."

Mr. Garcia wanted to call the police. "Dognapping is a serious crime!" he insisted.

But Mrs. Garcia said to wait. "Bear will turn up soon," she said. "It's past his dinnertime, and Bear is *always* hungry."

Mr. Patterson found Bear just after dark. He heard a noise in their garden shed, and there was Bear. Bear had food and water, and someone had fixed him a bed out of blankets and pillows. They were the Pattersons' blankets and pillows.

"You can't have him!" Leslie shrieked when Uncle Carlos took Bear from her father. "He belongs to me! I made a deposit! He can't go live in Michigan!"

Mr. Patterson tried to comfort Leslie. He put his arm around her shoulder and walked her through the Garcias' gate. "I'll make it up to you, Leslie. Come, see what I brought you from Pennsylvania."

But Leslie's sobs only got worse. Chad tried to block them out as he followed Mom and Dad home with Fudge in his arms. Leslie didn't want anything but Bear. And it was rotten rotten rotten that she couldn't have him.

12

That night Dad rewound the alarm clock while Mom refilled the hot-water bottle. Then he put them both in Fudge's bed. "Go to sleep, Fudge," he said. "And no more howling."

Chad put Wolfie in with Fudge. "She can't help it, Dad. You'd howl too if you had to sleep in the kitchen."

Mom laughed. "Your father howls if I steal his pillow."

Fudge *did* howl—and cry. It was worse than other nights. Chad heard Dad get up and close both the kitchen and bedroom doors. He covered his own ears with his pillow again. What was wrong with Fudge? Had Leslie's tantrum upset her? Did she know Bear was going to Michigan for good?

Then Chad *didn't* hear Fudge at all. He uncovered his ears and got up. He listened at his door. Nothing—not one whine. She's sick, he decided, and hurried through the house.

Fudge wasn't sick. She was chewing on Wolfie when Chad entered the kitchen. "Poor Wolfie," Chad said, and rescued his old toy. But Fudge continued chewing on something, and Chad scooped her out of the playpen. He pulled a piece of Wolfie's ear out of her mouth. "Bad girl," Chad scolded. "You could have choked."

Fudge snuggled against his shoulder, warm and soft. Chad didn't want to put her down. He wanted to take her to his room.

"You wouldn't puddle on my bed, would you?" Chad asked. "You wouldn't bark and wake everyone up?"

Fudge licked his chin and snuggled closer. "All right, but you have to be quiet!" Chad carried Fudge to his room and shut the door.

At first Fudge wanted to play. But when Chad crawled into bed, she lay down and curled against his knees.

Chad didn't plan to fall asleep—he meant to stay awake until *Fudge* fell asleep, then take her back to the kitchen. But he *was* asleep when Fudge stirred and woke him up. He felt something warm on his legs—something warm and wet.

"Oh, no!" Chad groaned. *Fudge had wet the bed!* He jumped out of bed and hurried Fudge back to the kitchen. He had to change the bed and wash the sheets before morning. He was getting clean sheets out of the hall closet when Dad turned on the light.

"Chad, what's going on?" Dad asked.

Chad thought of pretending *he'd* wet his own bed. But he told Dad the truth. "Fudge was crying, then she wasn't. She was eating Wolfie. I only wanted her to calm her."

Dad shook his head. "I'll help you change the bed and wash the wet sheets, Chad. And we'll talk about this tomorrow."

Mom woke up when Dad bumped the door with his arms full of wet bedding. She stepped into the hall rubbing her eyes. "John? Chad? Is something wrong?"

Chad tried to explain about Fudge chewing Wolfie. But Mom said he knew he was not supposed to take Fudge out of the playpen at night, no matter what.

"Go back to bed, Chad," Dad said.

Chad watched the curtains puff inward from the night breeze. Fudge's cries grew faint, and he hoped she was falling asleep. He hoped Leslie had stopped crying too. Even if it was dumb, he understood why she had dog-napped Bear.

In the morning Dad put the washed sheets in the dryer. Then he washed another load of dirty laundry while Chad took care of Fudge. "When the clothes are dry, take them out," Dad said. "Try to keep Fudge quiet, and stick around until your mother gets up."

Last night Dad had said, "We'll talk about this tomorrow." But Chad didn't remind him.

Chad took Fudge out, fed her, and took her out again. When the clothes were dry, he put Fudge in the playpen. Then he dumped the laundry on the dining-room table. Mom might cheer up if he folded everything before she got up.

Chad folded the towels in one pile and the T-shirts in another. He folded all the socks in pairs. It was easy—Dad's socks were black and Chad's were brown. Mom's socks were white with blue stripes on the cuffs and toes.

He was putting the towels away when Mom got up. Proudly he presented her with the matched and folded socks. "I folded everything," he said.

Mom took the socks and said, "So you're making points with good old Mom."

Chad followed her into the bedroom. "I'm sorry about last night. I won't take Fudge to bed again until you say—even if it's weeks and weeks."

Mom leaned on the dresser. "I know you're trying, Chad. And I know it isn't easy—taking care of Fudge. But that's what we told you when we made the agreement with Mr. Garcia."

Chad didn't want to hear any more and was glad when the telephone rang. It was Grandma Olsen calling long distance to talk to Mom.

Chad took Fudge out on the porch and plopped down on the steps. The agreement! The trial! He wished it were over and Fudge were positively theirs—once and for all.

Across the street Aunt Jessie and Uncle Carlos were getting ready to leave. Uncle Carlos loaded suitcases in the back of the van, and Aunt Jessie climbed in front with Bear.

All the Garcias were shouting, "Good-bye."

"There goes your brother," Chad said, pulling Fudge onto his lap. "Poor Leslie."

As soon as the van left, Tomas yelled across the street, "Chad! Wait until you hear!"

Immediately Tomas, Carmella, and Anna raced across Franklin Street together.

"Guess what! Guess what!" Anna shrieked.

They all piled onto the porch and Carmella explained. "Papa talked to Leslie's father last night. Mama talked to her mother this morning!"

"So?" Chad said impatiently.

"So they offered to sell them Bear on trial, like Fudge," Tomas said. "Until they know if Leslie's sister is allergic or not."

"And they both said yes!" Anna shouted. "Leslie gets to keep Bear."

Chad was confused. "But Aunt Jessie and Uncle Carlos—I saw them leave with Bear."

"With Figgie!" Tomas, Carmella, and Anna yelled at once.

"Tomas! Carmella! Anna!" Mrs. Garcia called. "If you want new shoes, we leave in five minutes!"

At once Tomas, Carmella, and Anna hurried home.

Chad was happy for Leslie—he could picture her cheering and laughing and shouting. But he wasn't happy for himself. He didn't want to wait until the week was over. He wanted to know about *keeping* Fudge—now!

Mom was sitting on a kitchen stool making sandwiches for lunch. "Egg salad, your favorite." She held out a spoon for a taste.

Chad shook his head as he put Fudge in the pen. Then he told Mom about Leslie and Bear. "Mom, I want to know about *Fudge*. Are we keeping her or not?"

"We've only had Fudge five days," Mom said. "The trial is for one week."

"I know," Chad said. "But I don't want to wait."

Mom nodded. "I understand. I hate waiting too, but let's just wait until Dad gets home."

That's when Chad decided to make a list of all the reasons they should keep Fudge. He headed the list "Reasons for Keeping Fudge."

Dad got home twenty minutes late. "These last-minute customers," he complained as he took off his jacket and sat down.

"I don't want to wait!" Chad blurted. "I want to know now—do we keep Fudge or not!"

"Chad is right," Mom said. "If we don't know by now . . ."

Chad placed his list in front of Dad. Then he lifted Fudge out of the playpen and held her tight.

" 'Reasons for Keeping Fudge,' " Dad read. Mom was trying not to smile.

" 'She is playful. She is cute. She chases ants and beetles.' " Dad took a breath. " 'Future Frisbee champion. Future watchdog.' This is some list, Chad." Then Dad cleared his throat and scratched his nose.

"Go on," Mom said. "Is there more?"

"One more," Dad said. He cleared his throat again. " 'The babies will love her.' "

"Oh, Chad," Mom said. She blew her nose and pulled Chad close. "The babies *will* love her. And I love her and you and the whole world."

Mom smelled like onions from the cabbage salad she was making for dinner. But Chad didn't pull away—even when his eyes started watering.

Dad said, "We've been so overwhelmed by the babies, Chad—we should have encouraged you more. You didn't give up or complain or forget to feed Fudge *once*."

Mom said, "And you understood when *I* complained, Chad. You didn't throw a tantrum or argue back."

Just then Leslie opened the back door without knocking and stepped in the kitchen. She was carrying Bear. "Big news! I get to keep Bear!" she announced.

Fudge barked when she saw Bear. "Big news!" Chad said. "I get to keep Fudge! Right, Dad—Mom?"

"Right!" Dad said, and Mom blew her nose again.

Chad put Fudge down on the floor. Leslie set Bear down too. "I came to ask—can Chad watch Bear on Monday? We're going to my sister's allergy doctor in the city. My father says we are keeping Bear—even if Jennifer has to take something so she won't sneeze."

Mom laughed, and Dad took Fudge's squeaky toy away from Bear.

"I charge for dog-sitting," Chad said. "Fifty cents an hour."

"You still owe *me* four dollars for watching Fudge!" Leslie argued.

"Three!" Chad said firmly.

Fudge bit Bear's tail. Bear leaped onto

Fudge's back. Leslie yelled, and Chad hollered.

Dad threw up his hands like a football referee. "Something tells me this is just the beginning," he groaned.

Mom dabbed her eyes with a paper towel. It was because of the onions. Chad knew they always made her cry.

About the Author

CHARLOTTE TOWNER GRAEBER is a confirmed
animal lover. She lives in Elgin, Illinois, with her
two dogs, Fritz and Fudge, and many kinds of
birds, including cockatoos and a macaw. She has
written many popular books about animals and
people, including *Grey Cloud* (a Friends of
American Writers Award winner) and *Mustard*
(an Irma Simonton Black Award winner).